EX LIBRIS

VINTAGE CLASSICS

THE LONELY SKIER

Ralph Hammond Innes was born in Horsham, Sussex, on 15 July 1913 and educated at Cranbrook School, Kent. He left school aged eighteen, and worked successively in publishing, teaching and journalism. In 1936, in need of money in order to marry, he wrote a supernatural thriller, *The Doppelganger*, which was published in 1937 as part of a two-year, four-book deal. In 1939 Innes moved to a different publisher, and began to write compulsively, continuing to publish throughout his service in the Royal Artillery during the Second World War.

Innes travelled widely to research his novels and always wrote from personal experience – his 1940s novels *The Blue Ice* and *The White South* were informed by time spent working on a whaling ship in the Antarctic, while *The Lonely Skier* came out of a post-war skiing course in the Dolomites. He was a keen and accomplished sailor, which passion inspired his 1956 bestseller *The Wreck of the Mary Deare*. The equally successful 1959 film adaptation of this novel enabled Innes to buy a large yacht, the *Mary Deare*, in which he sailed around the world for the next fifteen years, accompanied by his wife and fellow author Dorothy Lang.

Innes wrote over thirty novels, as well as several works of non-fiction and travel journalism. His thrilling stories of spies, counterfeiters, black markets and shipwreck earned him both literary acclaim and an international following, and in 1978 he was awarded a CBE. Hammond Innes died at his home in Suffolk on 10 June 1998.

HAMMOND INNES

The Lonely Skier

WITH AN INTRODUCTION BY
Stella Rimington

VINTAGE BOOKS
London

Published by Vintage 2013

2 4 6 8 10 9 7 5 3 1

First published in Great Britain by Collins in 1948

Vintage
Random House, 20 Vauxhall Bridge Road,
London SW1V 2SA

www.vintage-classics.info

Addresses for companies within The Random House Group Limited
can be found at: www.randomhouse.co.uk/offices.htm

The Random House Group Limited Reg. No. 954009

A CIP catalogue record for this book
is available from the British Library

ISBN 9780099577423

The Random House Group Limited supports the Forest Stewardship
Council® (FSC®), the leading international forest-certification organisation.
Our books carrying the FSC label are printed on FSC®-certified paper.
FSC is the only forest-certification scheme supported by the leading
environmental organisations, including Greenpeace. Our paper procurement
policy can be found at www.randomhouse.co.uk/environment

Set in Bembo
Typeset by Palimpsest Book Production Limited, Falkirk, Stirlingshire

Printed and bound in Great Britain by
Clays Ltd, St Ives PLC

To
PETER WILSON

This book will, I hope, recall many pleasant memories of places we have visited together. And because its setting is the Dolomites, it will particularly remind you of a little *albergo* near the Ponte nelle Alpi where we met for a drink. You were on your way up to Cortina. I was coming down from Cortina to Venice.

Aldbourne, 1946.

Introduction

The Second World War provided both the inspiration and the readership for a new wave of British thriller writers, of whom Hammond Innes was one. He and others such as Alistair MacLean, and later Ian Fleming, drew on their wartime experiences to set new standards of accuracy in their depiction of places and in the technical details underpinning their stories. They were writing at first for a predominantly male audience who to one degree or another shared those wartime experiences and demanded authenticity, a fast pace and hints of glamour not easily come by in the immediate post-war world. It was a readership facing unemployment and the very real possibility of a renewed World War. Perhaps that helps to explain an epic, almost fearful, element in Hammond Innes's writing, which it retained throughout his long career – he published his last novel in 1992.

Hammond Innes was the first of the new generation out of the trap. He had published several thrillers before the war and he wrote two more during the war, while he was serving in the Royal Artillery. None had attracted much critical attention, though he had shown what he could do in *Wreckers Must Breathe*, published in 1940 just before he joined the army. But it was not until 1947 and the publication of *The Lonely Skier* that he began to achieve favourable notice, and from then on his feet were set firmly on the path that would lead to his becoming the most wide-ranging and the longest lasting of all the post-war thriller writers. Four of his early books, including *The Lonely Skier*, were made into films, but it was not until he published his masterpiece,

The Wreck of the Mary Deare, in 1956 that he joined the ranks of the super-best-sellers and could buy his own ocean-going yacht to scour the world for new scenery and plots – and also to discover a new 'green' philosophy.

The Lonely Skier is not the classic tale of adventure that its title might suggest. Its main character, Neil Blair, who performs the role of commentator on the action, is an ordinary man who finds himself in an extraordinary situation. Demobbed, unemployed and penniless, he stumbles on a job with the vaguest of briefs: to go to a mountain hut, a *rifigio* on Col da Varda above Cortina in the Italian Dolomites, to pretend to be writing a film script and to watch and report what happens. He finds himself cooped up in the *rifigio*, to which the only access is via a 'slit-tovia', a dodgy-sounding cable sleigh, with an assorted bunch of suspicious-looking Europeans. Who are they and why are they there? This is not so much a whodunnit as a who-dun what and why? The tale develops out of past relationships, only gradually disclosed to the reader, coupled with a good deal of retrospective wartime skulduggery, with the hero when he eventually arrives acting as a catalyst, forcing the situation into the open.

If this sounds like a plot that Agatha Christie might have produced, I am doing it a grave injustice. It is far more than that. This plot is woven from the torn fabric of post-war Europe. As one of the characters observes, it is 'a strange, sick Europe . . . Beyond men and women here who have grown fat on war, there is a vast human jungle . . . It is the survival of the fittest.' Hammond Innes creates a small piece of that human jungle inside the *rifigio*.

The ordinary man who finds himself in extraordinary circumstances is a theme beloved of one of Hammond Innes's contemporaries, writing just before the war, Eric Ambler. But whereas Ambler sets his plots in the throbbing heat of the Côte d'Azur, Hammond Innes chooses for this novel the freezing snowfields, glaciers and high passes of the Dolomites. It is not only the human jungle that has to be confronted and conquered but the mighty forces of nature. The idea of man versus nature is a constant theme in Innes's stories. In *Wreckers Must Breathe* it is the subterranean world of caves – the silence, the darkness and the risks of flooding and subsidence – that must be faced. Often, as in *The Blue Ice,* published a year after *The Lonely Skier,* it is the sea in all its moods. But in *The Lonely Skier* it is the sea's opposite, the mountains, and all the fearful difficulties and obstacles that high altitudes can produce and that man must overcome by skill, perseverance and daring.

Though his attitudes and concerns were to change and become wider with the expansion of his readership and the trend of world events, Innes continued to be fascinated by the idea of man confronted by the forces of nature. But in his attitude to that struggle he eventually switched sides. In the earlier books, and *The Lonely Skier* is one example, it is heroic for man to face nature's obstacles and overthrow them through his human qualities as well as his skill. Later in his life, Innes saw Man as 'a rogue species and doomed', a violent creature whose 'will to conquer is invincible' but whose egotism and greed are destroying the balances of nature. 'Man is a killer and he carries the seed of his own destruction', and 'the world seems to be shrieking aloud at the cruelty of humans'. His later heroes have the task of exposing, challenging and resisting the consequences of follies to which they themselves are prone. And all along, in the earlier as well as in the later books, the hero is a lonely man driven by a mission in the course of which he self-destructs.

Nor are Innes's heroes all particularly nice people. The true hero in *The Lonely Skier* is not Neil Blair, the ordinary man; Blair is instead the observer, the commentator. The hero is the man who gives him the job, Engles, a former British Military Intelligence officer. Engles could be 'a cruel, sneering devil', cool, insolent to his friends and enemies alike, and incidentally, with a style rather too direct for a spy. His *savoir faire* is impeccable, but he himself confesses that 'pride . . . and my insatiable desire for excitement' are what drive him on. His upper lip remains at all times stiff: 'I didn't mean to land you in a mess like this. Make no mistake about it, Neil – we're in a pretty tight spot' – rather an understatement in the context. A whole phalanx of fictional British heroes from Richard Hannay to Dick Barton would have applauded the words, though they would not have approved of Innes's habit of killing his heroes.

Though women play a quite considerable part in his dramas, on the whole, Innes's heroes are misogynists and his narrators, who, as in *The Lonely Skier*, are usually distinct from the heroes, are only marginally less so. In *The Blue Ice* the narrator actually marries, or at least lives with a woman who fully shares his perils, just as Innes's own wife shared his wanderings about the oceans in search of locations for his plots. Carla, the only significant woman in *The Lonely Skier*, is a nasty piece of work – 'all of a man's baser thoughts come true' – who gets her come-uppance at the hands of her serially murderous lover. In other respects she resembles other of Innes's female characters in having too wide a mouth for conventional good looks. Readers looking for feminine interest or steamy sex will be disappointed.

His real love is landscape and seascape both in its grand sweep and in the vivid depiction of its tiny appearances. *The Lonely Skier* is full of both: the 'wind . . . took hold of the trees and shook them like a terrier shakes a rat. The snow fell in great slabs from their whipping branches . . . the wind . . . driving the snowflakes almost horizontal to the ground'. His scenes of skiing and sailing are wholly convincing in the same accurate, mind-catching detail of their small touches, and also in their treatment of natural phenomena and scenery in all their awesome majesty. Up in the high pass 'the dark peaks jostled one another, battling to be the first to pierce the heavens, and all about them their snow skirts dropped away to the world below, the nice comfortable world where human beings lived.'

As with Eric Ambler before him, Innes took immense trouble to get his technical details right. In his own foreword to *The Blue Ice*, set largely in Norway, he tells us that 'it was necessary for me to go over the entire ground including the long trek from Aurland to Finse over the Sankt Paal glacier'. For the same book he took a job in a vilely smelly whale-meat factory and completed his first serious trip in an ocean racer. In *The Lonely Skier* the skiing sequences are very clearly based on his personal experience both of the terrain and of the finer arts of the sport, learned on an army skiing course he took shortly before writing the book. He applies his knowledge to building the tension towards a murderous and eminently plausible climax, and to expressing the fear of death, taking the reader with him all the way in a vivid description of the accident that ends a tremendously fast descent down a steep mountainside.

> The snow slope beyond flung itself at me. A cold, wet world closed about me in an icy smother . . . I sobbed for the air I needed . . . Then the grey light of the sky showed through a hole in the snow . . . The truth dawned on me slowly as I lay there in the snow. [He] *had meant this to happen.*

Similarly Innes studied official procedures very closely, as demonstrated in his mastery of the court scene in *Mary Deare* and of maritime insurance procedures for his later books, and he is scrupulously fair to the officials involved. This care to get atmosphere and background right is his great strength, lending conviction to his narratives, a trait which he shares with contemporaries such as Fleming, later with le Carré, and which culminates in Frederick Forsyth – the latter, like Fleming and Innes, a journalist by training.

Innes is always readable and his earlier books rank very high as taut, fast-moving, page-turning tales of adventure, marked by strong elements of inevitability and self-compulsion. But he is more than just a thriller writer; he is essentially a moralist. Human motives and relationships matter more to him than individual personalities or even situations. For him, villainy begins with egotism and takes the form of cruelty and greed. The concerns and fears for the planet which he developed later in his life and his scepticism about the motives of business and governments spring from the same idea. Though he wrote of heroes and lived his own life on a heroic scale, he understood that heroism can be a form of egotism and serve evil as well as good. In *The Lonely Skier*, one of the more intelligent of the assorted bunch of villains in the *rifugio* says to Engels, 'We should help each other . . . these [other] people . . . are only interested for themselves . . . Whereas you and I, we have a mission.' The words, spoken by a crook, contain a warning. Heroism has two sides and only one of them is good.

Stella Rimington, 2013

1

A Journey to the Dolomites

I had seen all the rushes of the film, but it was the first time I had sat through the full cut version. The rushes had been pure routine, short slashes of film to be viewed critically for alterations and cuts. They had meant no more to me than pages torn at random from a manuscript. They were strips of celluloid to be cold-bloodedly hammered into shape.

But this was different—to sit there in the dark of the Studios' theatre and have the whole grim story retold on the screen. It wasn't, of course, exactly the way it had happened. It couldn't be. No audience would have stood for it told that way. We had twisted it about a good deal to make a straight story of it. But it was all there, so that, with a bag of sticky sweets and hot hands clasped in the dark, any one with a couple of bob to spare could lose themselves for an hour and twenty-three minutes and live in the atmosphere of tension and fear in which we had lived in that chalet in the heart of the Dolomites.

The film opened with an approaching shot of the chalet from the *slittovia*, just as I had seen it that first time. And as the cable sleigh neared the chalet, I lost all critical sense in my absorption in the story. For I knew what the inside of the hut would look like before the camera planed in through the window. I knew who would be there and what they would be saying. I sat and lived the story all over again.

You may say—how could I help knowing who would be there and what they would be saying since I had written the script? That is true. But it is one thing to make up a story; quite another to have written of things that actually happened—written with the dead, so to speak, looking over my shoulder. It was Engles' idea—to film a thriller that had really happened. He it was who had introduced me to the characters, helped to set the stage and had had a large part in directing the events of the story. He had even given me the title—typed it out in black and white with fingers already grown stiff and cold. The fact that I had written the script and another man had directed the film did not prevent it from seeming somehow entirely his work.

Thus, to me, the final version had something of a nightmare quality. And as the story I knew so well unfolded, each character on the screen transformed itself in the sockets of my brain and took on new features—features I had known. It was not the actors playing their parts that I saw, but the real people as they had once been. It was like a parade of ghosts. So many of them were dead. And I had come so near to death myself out there on the cold snow slopes below Monte Cristallo.

The story was so vivid in my mind. I did not need thousands of feet of film made at a cost of over £100,000 to recall it. Let the dead lie buried, not march like pale spectres out of a strip of celluloid, mouthing words they had once uttered when they were flesh and blood. It was unnatural and somehow rather horrible to sit there in a comfortable seat and see the whole thing neatly tied up with box office ticket ribbons ready for sale to the public.

This must sound a pretty strange opening to a story that has nothing of ghosts in it, but which tells of an ill-assorted group of people, of greed and violence in a strange setting. If I have begun at the wrong end, it is because it was after seeing the neat little parcel we had made of the film that I had the urge to tell the story exactly as it happened to me. I don't want to see the film again—ever. However big a success it is—and it has all the ingredients of success—I have seen all I want to see of it. Now I'll tell the story once and for all just as it happened. Then perhaps my mind will be exhausted with the telling of it and I shall be able to forget all about it.

Like most of the more startling events in life, I stumbled into it quite by chance. It was the First of December—a grey, wet day that fitted my mood—and it was in a chemist's shop of all places. Derek Engles was standing at the dispensing counter, drinking a dark fizzy pick-me-up out of a beaker. He caught my eye over the rim of it and frowned. He always liked people to believe that drink had no effect on his constitution. He took liquor like most people take food. His brain worked best that way. Everything he did and said had to be whipped up, and drink was the stimulant. He never ate breakfast and cured his hangovers by secretly consuming aspirin, which he always carried about with him.

I don't know why he was in Shaftesbury Avenue that morning. It was just one of those things that happen. Sometimes Fate puts on a kindly mask and shakes up the pieces so that the right ones meet at the right moment. This was one of those occasions.

They say that things always work out for the best. But people who make that statement are always lapped in smug security at the time. I agree that life is cumulative and that the threads of each defined period of a man's life are woven into the pattern. But it is not always possible to pick up the right thread just at the moment when you need it most. And I was feeling pretty desperate when I met Engles.

Before the war I had had a nice little family business—a local paper in Wiltshire. But that went under and when I had been overseas three years and became due for release, I found I had no job to go back to. I was longing to get back to Peggy and the kid, but we agreed there was nothing for it but to sign on for another year. Then a friend of mine suggested starting up a publishing business in Exeter. He asked me to join him in the venture. When I came out we put all we had into it. It lasted six months—the paper shortage and lack of capital were too much for us.

I wrote to everyone I knew—people I had known before the war and contacts I had made in the Army. I combed the 'Situations Vacant' columns of the papers. But there were too many of us in the same boat. I sent Peggy and Michael back to our cottage in Wiltshire and here I was in London in search of a job.

It was five years since I had seen London, and in the meantime I had been halfway round the world. I had run big towns in Italy and Austria. I had lived in the best hotels in Europe. I had had servants and transport. And that morning I stood in the rain in Piccadilly Circus, an unimportant molecule in the great flood of London, feeling alone and a little lost. I was excited and at the same time depressed. Excited, because London is an exciting place. From Westminster to the City you can climb dingy stairs to offices whose ramifications cover the entire living globe. Anything is possible in London. The whole world seems to be under your hand. If you have the right contact and are the right man for the job, London holds the key to every country in the world. But I was also depressed, for there is no city in which you can feel so small and lonely and lost as London, especially if you have no job.

But because I needed some toothpaste as well as a job, I strolled up Shaftesbury Avenue and walked into the first chemist's I saw. And there was Engles.

I had been his Battery Captain back in 1942. We had gone overseas together. But after Alamein, he had transferred to the Intelligence and I had taken the Battery into Italy and had finished up as a Town Major. He had been an exacting Battery Commander. He had broken my two predecessors and everyone had said that I wouldn't last six weeks. But I had. I had even enjoyed working with him. He had been brilliant, moody and erratic. But he had an exciting personality and terrific drive and energy when things were difficult. Now he was back in films and, according to the papers, his directing of K. M. Studios' latest production, *The Three Tombstones*, had put him right at the top.

He nodded casually at my greeting, put the empty beaker down on the counter and looked hard at me for a moment as I made my purchase.

'What are you doing now, Neil?' he asked at length. He had a quick abrupt way of speaking as though his tongue worked too slowly for his mind.

'I haven't been back very long,' I told him. I had heard him sneer at failure too often to let him know the truth.

'Demobilised?'

'Yes.'

'You've been in a long time, haven't you?'

'Yes. I signed on for an extra year.'

'A good-time Charlie, eh?' he jeered.

'I don't get you,' I said. But I knew what he meant. Living conditions had been pretty good at the end—much better than at home.

He gave a harsh laugh. 'You know very well what I mean. All the bright boys were getting out when I left nearly eighteen months ago. The only ones staying on, apart from the regulars, were the duds and the adventurers—and the good-time Charlies. That's what is wrong with our European administration. There's no real future in the job, so it doesn't appeal to the sort of men we ought to have out there. Well, which category do you put yourself in?'

'Of the three categories you mention,' I replied, 'I think I'd prefer to be classed among the adventurers.' My voice sounded sullen. I couldn't help it. I was angry. I wasn't going to tell him how I had hated signing on for that extra year, when I had seen so little of Peggy since we had been married and had barely seen the kid since he had been born. And I felt uncomfortable, too. In the old days I had managed to stand up to Engles; not because my personality was as strong as his, but because I knew my job. But to face up to his volatile and domineering personality now,

5

when things were going badly, was too much. I wanted to rush out of that shop before he pried too deeply into my circumstances.

'And now you're back,' he said. 'Still running that tupenny ha'penny little rag down in Wiltshire?'

'No, that went smash,' I told him.

His dark eyes were watching me closely. 'Then what are you doing now?'

'I started a small publishing house with a friend,' I replied. 'What about you—are you working on another film now?'

But he wasn't to be put off so easily. 'It needs a lot of money to start up in publishing these days,' he said, still watching me. 'A whole crop of them sprang up like mushrooms soon after the war. They're mostly in difficulties now.' He hesitated. Then suddenly he gave me a queer puckish smile. He could be charming. He could turn it on like a tap. He could also be a cruel, sneering devil. But suddenly, there was the well-remembered smile and I felt a great relief as I realised that, despite his hangover, it was to be charm this morning. 'I think you need a drink,' he said. 'I know I do after that filthy stuff.' And he took my arm and led me out of the shop. As we crossed the road, he said, 'Done any more writing, Neil? Those two one-act plays of yours I produced on the ship going out—they weren't bad, you know.'

'I wrote a play whilst I was in Austria,' I told him. 'But you know what the theatre has been like—nothing but musicals and revivals. Even established playwrights can't get a theatre. And anyway, I doubt if it was good enough.'

'You sound as miserable as hell,' he said. 'Life is fun. Don't take it so seriously. Something always turns up at the last moment. Do you want a job?'

I stopped then. I could have hit him. His unfailing instinct for a man's weakness had told him I hadn't got a job and he was going to enjoy my discomfort. He was ruthless, unscrupulous. How he hated failure! How he revelled in attacking any man at his weakest point! It was incredible how that Welsh intuition of his smelled out a man's weakness. 'Life may be fun,' I said angrily. 'But it isn't as funny as all that.'

'Come on to the pavement,' he said. 'It's a lot safer. So you think I'm not serious?'

'I think you're behaving stupidly,' I snapped back at him. I was goaded by the thought that I had worked with this man on terms of equality and now he was in a position to cast me crumbs for the amusement of watching my reactions.

He took my arm in a firm grip and steered me through the glass door of a long gin palace of a saloon bar. He ordered whiskies. 'Here's fun!' he said, and raised his glass mockingly at me. He was laughing. It showed in his eyes. 'You think I'm not serious, eh?' he said. 'I am, you know—quite serious. Do you want a job or not?'

I downed my whisky at a gulp and ordered another round. 'I don't want your charity or your sneers,' I said. I was feeling very bitter.

'My God! You're prickly,' he said. 'But then you always were. Did you ever know me charitable? I seem to remember you telling me—more than once—that I was the most ruthless person you had ever met. Just because I wouldn't stand incompetence. It's a strange thing, but just at the moment I can't think of any one I would rather have run into. But life's like that. If you want a job done, the right man always turns up at the last minute. There are only about a half-dozen men I met in the Army who would be right for a job I have in mind. And if they'd all applied for it in a bunch, I'd have picked on you without a moment's hesitation.' The build-up was obvious. But I began to be interested. Engles never bothered to build any one up unless he really wanted to make use of them. He gave me a sudden warm smile. 'You know—I'm quite serious, Neil. If you want a job, I'd be glad to have you work with me again.'

'What sort of a job is it?' I asked.

'Three months at Cortina in the Dolomites as a script writer

7

for K. M. Studios,' he replied quickly. 'A hundred pounds a month and all expenses.'

I gasped. It was the chance of a lifetime and I had walked bang into it in a chemist's shop. But why me? 'What makes you think I can produce the sort of script you want?' I asked him.

'I don't want you to produce a script. I've got one already.'

'Then what in the world do you want me to do?'

He reacted immediately to my disappointment. He patted my shoulder. 'Three months in the finest ski-ing country in Europe isn't a bad offer,' he said.

'I know,' I said hastily. 'But I couldn't help being disappointed. You offer me a job as a script writer, and then you say you don't want a script. You know I always wanted to be a writer.'

'I didn't mean to disappoint you,' he said. 'Look, Neil. It's best to be frank with you. I don't think you could write the sort of film script I want. But if you do write one, I'll promise you this—I'll read it and if I can use it in preference to the one I've got, I will. That's fair, eh?'

'Very fair,' I agreed. 'Now, what do you really want me to do?'

'You speak Italian, don't you?' he asked.

'Enough to get around,' I replied.

'Good!' He smiled. 'Since you class yourself among the adventurers, you might find this quite amusing. On the other hand, it may be a complete wash-out. In which case you will have to be content with three months' holiday in the Dolomites. It's just a hunch I have about something. I can't follow it up myself. I'm finishing off my next film. What I need is somebody I can trust to hold a watching brief for me and keep me informed—somebody with a sense of responsibility and plenty of initiative. You're just the man.'

'Thanks for the build-up,' I said. I was becoming excited despite my previous disappointment. Engles' excitement was always infectious.

He laughed. 'That's not a build-up. You just happen to possess those qualities. You can also write, and that gives me a pretext for sending you out. Now—do you want the job?'

'Well, what is the job?' I asked him.

'For God's sake, Neil!' he cried. 'Do you want it or don't you?'

'Of course I do,' I replied. 'I need a job badly. But naturally I want to know what the job is. How else can I tell whether I can do it?'

'You should know me better,' he said in a quieter tone. 'I wouldn't be offering you the job if I didn't think you could do it. Now, are you going to take it or not?'

'I'd like to,' I said.

'Fine!' And he ordered another round before I was halfway through my own drink. 'Just a final,' he said, 'whilst I tell you what I want you to do. Then I must dash or I'll miss my train. Do you know Cortina?'

I shook my head. I knew of it, of course. We had taken it over as a leave centre for our troops at the end of the war.

'Doesn't matter,' he went on. 'I plan to do a film there. There's not enough movement in modern films. Too much of the play about them. That's why Westerns are so popular. The studios seem to think people go to the cinema to listen. They don't. They go to watch. There's a colossal market waiting for a fast-moving ski picture. Plenty of spills and thrills. The world has gone crazy about sport—artificial excitement to replace the excitement of war. But I've got to convince my Studios first. I'm sending a fat, sluggish ape called Joe Wesson, who happens to be a first-class cameraman, over to take some pictures that will convince K. M. Studios that I'm right. You'll go with him to do the script. That's just an excuse to get you the permit. I don't give a damn whether you write a script or not, but you'd better try. Joe Wesson will expect it. To everyone else but me you're there to write a script. You'll be on the Studios' pay-roll as a script writer. I'll fix that.'

He lit a cigarette. 'You'll stay at a place called Col da Varda,' he went on. 'It's about five miles north of Cortina. It's little more than a *rifugio*, but it's got bedrooms. I've booked accommodation for two already. You go up to the Passo Tre Croci and take a cable sleigh—*slittovia*, the Ityes call them—up to the hut. Make a pretence of writing and watch everyone who comes up there. Particularly, watch for this girl.' He produced a photograph from his wallet and handed it to me.

It was a very faded and much-worn photograph of the head and undraped shoulders of a girl. It had been taken in Berlin and scrawled across the bottom was—'*Für Heinrich, mein liebling — Carla.*' 'She's Italian,' he said. I could see that. She had dark hair and eyes and a wide full mouth. There was something very animal about that face and the eyes had a glittering hardness. It reminded me of some of the pictures of girls I had seen in the Vice Squad's index of prostitutes shortly after the fall of Rome.

'Understand, I don't want you to do anything,' Engles continued. 'I just want you to keep your eyes open. I'm interested in the *slittovia* and the hut, the people who are staying there, regular visitors, anything unusual that happens. I'm not going to tell you anything about it. If you keep your eyes and ears open, you'll probably come to know as much about the business as I do. But, *I don't want you to do anything*. Send me a daily report. If there's anything startling, cable me at the Studios. Send your reports Air Mail. Is all that clear?'

'As mud,' I said.

He grinned. 'That's about as clear as I wanted it to be. See my secretary tomorrow. She'll fix everything for you.' He glanced at his watch and drained his drink. 'I'll just make it,' he said. 'It'll be a three months' engagement and, if my hunch turns out right, you might find yourself nicely set up. At worst you might produce a script I could use. You leave for Cortina the day after tomorrow.'

With that he clapped me on the back and hurried out, leaving me slightly bewildered, but feeling suddenly that the world was an exciting place and life worth living again. Here was a chance to write a film script handed me on a platter. I had several more drinks at that bar, savouring the excitement of the moment with the warmth of the whisky. If I wrote a script—and it were good enough—Engles, I knew, would keep his word. I did not spare much thought for the private assignment he had given me. I did not know then that it was to oust from my mind any thought of writing a script until I wrote of the actual events that occurred at Col da Varda.

When I got back to the cottage that night Peggy met me at the door and she saw at once that our luck had turned. Her face lit up. We laughed together over the strangeness of it all and went out to celebrate, spending money without thought for the first time in months, planning the script I should write. The fact that we were to be separated again didn't seem to matter. It was for a short time and we were people with a future if we could grasp hold of it.

So it was that, two days later, I found myself sharing a carriage with Joe Wesson. Engles' description of him as 'a fat, sluggish ape' was cruel, but not inappropriate. He had heavy features. The skin below the sockets of his eyes was dragged down by great pouches. His cheeks swept in ample folds to his splendid chins and flapped like dewlaps as he talked. He weighed, I should guess, over fifteen stone. He was, in fact, one of the most impressive figures I have ever seen and to watch him fitting himself into his sleeping berth was as good as a visit to the panda's cage at the London Zoo.

He was in a furious temper when he joined me on the platform at Victoria. He had a hangover and obviously hated travel. 'You're Neil Blair, are you?' he said. He was panting, but for all that he was quick enough on his feet. 'I'm Joe Wesson. We've been had for a couple of mugs, blast Engles' God-damned soul! Why couldn't he convince the Studios himself without sending us to shiver on a Dolomite, taking pictures and writing scripts?'

He heaved his gear on to the rack. 'The Studios will do what he says anyway. He could just as well talk them into it. He's got a tongue, and 'tisn't as though it's rusty. But he must have the whole circus running around full of the same idea.' He fitted himself into a corner seat facing the engine and, as though to bear out Engles' theories, brought out a stack of Westerns, picked up the top one and settled himself to read.

He worked his way steadily down through that pile of Westerns as we crossed the Channel and the train rattled across France and through Switzerland—that is, when he wasn't taking on food or drink, both of which he did noisily and in large quantities, or when he wasn't sleeping, which he did even more noisily, snoring with a strange series of grunts that ended in a slight long-drawn-out whistle.

He didn't talk much. But once he leaned across in a friendly way and said, 'New to the K.M. set-up, aren't you, old man?' He had a queer way of jerking his sentences out as though he were always short of breath. When I told him I was, he shook his head so that his cheeks quivered. 'Good firm when you're on top, but God help you when you're not. They're a hard lot. Can't afford to make a mistake with them. If you do—' he snapped his fingers expressively—'you're finished. Engles is their big man at the moment. He may last one year. He may last five. Worked with him before?'

I told him what my previous association with Engles was. 'Ah!' he said. 'Then you probably know him better than I do. Get to know men when you live with them like that. He can be charming. And then again he can be a devil. Most ruthless director I ever worked with. If a star doesn't toe the line, they're out—he'll get a new star or make one. That's how Lyn Barin jumped to fame in *The Three Tombstones*. The original star was Betty Carew. She threw a fit of temperament—wanted scenes played her own way. Engles chucked her off the set. His language was a poem in technicolour. Next day he had the Barin girl there. No one had ever heard of her. And he made her a star right there on the set. He got the acting he wanted and the film was the better for it. Betty Carew had done good work for K.M. But she's washed up now.' He heaved a sigh. 'Why you blokes ever come out of the Army, God knows! You're safe there. Nobody can throw you out unless you do something stupid.' Then he suddenly smiled. His smile was quite delightful. His face, for all its loose flesh, was strangely expressive. 'Still, I admit I wouldn't change places with 'em. Life's a fight anyway. There's no fun in knowing you're safe whether your work is good or bad.' And he returned with a deep sigh of contentment to his Westerns.

It was dark and the snow was falling when we arrived at Cortina. Once out of the lights of the station our sense of pleasure at having finished the journey was damped by the blanket of steadily falling snow. The soft sound of it was audible in the still night. It hid the lights of the little town and muffled the chained wheels of the hotel bus.

Cortina is like all winter sports' resorts. It is a veneer of civilisation's luxuries planted by hotel-keepers in the heart of a wild country of forests, snow and jagged peaks. Because of the lateness of our arrival, we had arranged to stay the first night at the Splendido and go on up to Col da Varda the next day.

As soon as we passed through the Splendido's swing doors, the glittering palace lapped its luxury round us like a hot bath. In every room central heating thrust back the cold of the outside world. There were soft lights, dance bands, and the gleam of silver. Italian waiters, with a hundred different drinks, threaded their way through a colourful mob of men and women from a dozen different countries. Everything was laid on—ski instructors, skating instructors, transport to the main runs, ice hockey matches, ski jumping. It was like a department store in which the thrills of the snow country can be bought at so much a yard. And outside the snow fell heavily.

I picked up a pile of brochures on Cortina whilst waiting for dinner. One announced it as 'the sunny snow paradise in the Dolomites.' Another became lyrical over the rocky peaks, describing them as 'pinnacles rising out of the snow and looking like flames mounting into the Blue Sky.' They spoke with awe of fifty-eight different ski runs and, referring to summer sport at Cortina, stated, 'it is almost impossible to be tired at Cortina: Ride before breakfast, golf before lunch, tennis in the afternoon and a quick bath before dressing for dinner—still one is ready to dance until the early hours.' Nothing out of the ordinary could happen here, I felt. They had made a playground of the cold snow, and the grim Dolomite bastions were pretty peaks to be admired at sunset with a dry Martini.

Joe Wesson had something of the same reaction. He suddenly materialised at my elbow. He wore rubber-soled shoes and moved quietly for such a large man. 'Not a hair out of place, eh?' he said, looking at the brochure over my shoulder. 'It's like the Italians to try to tame Nature with a pot of brilliantine. But it can't be far from here that twenty thousand men died trying to get Hannibal's elephants through the passes. And only a year or two back, I suppose, a lot of our blokes were frozen to death attempting to get through from Germany.'

I tossed the brochures back on to the pile. 'It might be Palm Beach, or the Lido, Venice, or Mayfair,' I agreed. 'Same people—same atmosphere. Only I suppose it's all white outside.'

He gave a snort of disgust and led the way into dinner.

'You'll be glad enough to return to it,' he muttered, 'after you've had a day or two up in that damned hut.'

As I sat down, I glanced round the room at the other diners, wondering whether the girl who had signed herself 'Carla' in that photograph would be there. She wasn't, of course, though the majority of the women in the room were Italian. I wondered why Engles should expect her to be at Cortina.

'No need to try and catch their eyes,' Joe Wesson said through

14

a mouthful of *ravioli*. 'Judging by the looks of most of 'em, you've only got to leave your bedroom door open.'

'You're being unnecessarily coarse,' I said.

His little bloodshot eyes twinkled at me. 'Sorry, old man. Forgot you'd been in Italy long enough to know your way around. Is it a *contessa* or a *marchesa* you're expecting?'

'I don't quite know,' I replied. 'It could just as well be a *signora*, or even a *signorina*, or just a common or garden little tart.'

'Well, if it's the last you're wanting,' he said, 'you shouldn't have much difficulty in this assembly.'

After dinner I went in search of the owner of the hotel. I wanted to find out what local information I could about Col da Varda and its *slittovia*. Our accommodation at the chalet had been booked through him and I thought, therefore, that he should be able to tell me what there was to know.

Edouardo Mancini was a short stocky man of very light colouring for an Italian. He was part Venetian and part Florentine and he had lived a long time in England. In fact, he had once been in the English bob-sleigh team. He had been among the great of the bob-sleigh world. But he had had to pack it up ten years ago after a really bad smash. His right arm had been broken in so many places that it was virtually useless.

Once he had doubtless been a slim, athletic figure, but when I met him he had put on weight so that his movements were slow. He was a heavy drinker. I imagine that started after his final accident. It was not difficult to pick him out among his guests. He looked almost a cripple, his big body moving slowly, almost stiffly among them. He had broken practically every bone in his body at one time or another and I believe he carried quite a weight of platinum around in place of missing bone. But in spite of this, his rather dissipated features were genial under his mop of titian hair, which rose almost straight up from his scalp, giving him height and a curiously youthful air. He was a very wealthy man and the biggest hotelier in Cortina.

Most of this I learned from an American I had met in the bar before dinner. He had been a Colonel in the American Army and had had something to do with Cortina when it was being run as an Allied leave centre.

I found Edouardo Mancini in the bar. He and his wife were having a drink with my American friend and two British officers up from Padua. The American introduced me. I mentioned that I was going up to Col da Varda the next day. 'Ah, yes,' Mancini said. 'There are two of you—no? And you are planning to do a film? You see, I know who my guests are.' And he beamed delightedly. He spoke English very fast and with just the trace of a Cockney accent mixed up with the Italian intonation. But it was very difficult to follow him, for his speech was obstructed by saliva which crept into the corners of his mouth as he talked. I imagine his jaw had been smashed up in one of his accidents and had not set properly.

'Col da Varda belongs to the hotel, does it?' I asked.

'No, no—good heavens, no!' He shook his large head vehemently. 'You must not have that idea. I would not like you to blame all the short-comings of the place on me. You would obtain a bad impression. My hotel is my home. I do not have *anybody* here, you understand. You are my guests. That is the way I like to think of all these people.' And he waved his hand towards the colourful crowd that thronged the bar and lounge. 'If anything is wrong, we look at it as you would say, my wife and I, we are bad hosts. That is why I will not have you accuse me of Col da Varda. It is not comfortable there. That Aldo is a fool. He does not know how to arrange people. He is lazy and, most terrible of all, he is no good for the bar. Is that not so, Mimosa?'

His wife nodded and smiled from behind her Martini. She was small and attractive and had a nice smile.

'I will—how you say it?—sack him. Please excuse my English.

16

It is many years since I was in England. I had hotels in Brighton and London. But that was long before the war.'

I assured him that he spoke excellent English. Indeed, if I had spoken Italian as well in my own country I should not have felt impelled to apologise.

He nodded, as though that were the reply he expected. 'Yes, I will give him the sack.' He turned to his wife. 'We will give him the sack, dear, the day after tomorrow and we will put Alfredo there. He has a good wife and they will run it well.' He put his hand on my arm. 'In the meantime, you will not blame me—yes? I am only what your doctors would call *in locum parentis* at the moment. I do the bookings. But on Friday it will become a little piece of the Splendido. Then, if you stay long, you will remark a difference. But it will take time, you understand?'

'You mean you are taking it over?' I asked.

He nodded. 'On Friday. There is an auction. I shall buy it. It is all arranged. Then you will see.'

'I don't quite get you, Mancini,' said the American. 'Don't you have to bid at an Italian auction? A thing like that, auctioned in America, would attract all sorts of real-estators and business men who'd enjoy running a toy like a *slittovia*. I know you're the biggest hotelier in the place. But I guess there are others who might like that little property.'

'You do not understand,' Mancini said with a quick crinkling of the eyes. 'We are not fools here. We are business men. And we are not like the cats and dogs. We arrange things with order-liness. The others do not want it. It is too far out for them. But I have a very big hotel here and I am always progressive. It will make money because Col da Varda will become the Splendido's own ski run. I shall run a bus service and it will not be crowded like the Pocol, Tofana and Faloria runs. So, no one will bid but me. An outsider would never buy. He knows there would be a boycott.'

'I'd like to see an Italian auction,' I said. 'Where is it being held?'

'In the lounge of the Luna. You really wish to come?'

'Yes,' I told him. 'It would be very interesting.'

'Then you shall come with me—yes?' Mancini shook his head, smiling. 'But it will be very dull, you know. No fireworks. There will be just the one bid—a very low one. And then it will be over. But if you really wish to come, meet me here at a quarter to eleven on Friday and we will go together. After, we will have a little drink to celebrate—also because, if I do not give you a drink, then you will feel the time is wasted.' He gave a deep throaty chuckle. 'The Government will make little out of it. Which is good because we do not like the Government here. It is of the south and we have a preference for Austria, you know. We are Italian, but we found the Austrians governed better. If there were a plebiscite, I think this part of the country would vote to return to Austria.'

'What's the Government got to do with it?' asked the American. 'As I remember it, the *slittovia* was constructed by the Germans for their Alpine troops. Then a British division took it over. Did the British Military sell out to the Italian Government?'

'No, no. When the war was nearly over, the Germans sold it cheap to the man who once owned the Excelsiore. It was from him that the *slittovia* was requisitioned by the British. His hotel was requisitioned, too. But when the British left, he found it difficult. He had been too great a collaborator. We persuaded him that it would be best to sell and a small syndicate of us bought him out. You see, we are quite a little family here in Cortina. If things are not right, we make adjustments. That was a year ago. Business was not good, you know. We did not want the *slittovia* then. It was sold very cheap to a man named Sordini.' He made a dramatic pause. 'That was a strange business—eh? We did not know. How could we? He was a stranger. It was a big surprise to us when he was arrested. And the two workmen he had up there—they were Germans, too.'

'I don't understand,' I said, trying to hide my excitement. 'Was this Sordini a German?'

'But yes,' he said in a tone of surprise. 'The name Sordini was an *alias*. He took it in order to escape just retribution for all his crimes. It was all in the papers. It was even on your own radio—I heard it myself. It was a captain of the *carabinieri* who arrested him. The captain and I were drinking together here in this bar the night before he went up to the hut. We think Sordini must have bought the place as a hideout. They took him to Rome and put him in the Regina Coeli. But he did not kill himself in that prison. Oh no—probably he had friends and hoped to escape, like Roatta, Mussolini's commander in Albania, who was reported to have strolled out of the prison hospital in his pyjamas and got away down the Tiber in a miniature submarine. No, it was when he was handed over to the British to join the rest of the war criminals that he took the poison.'

'What was his real name?' My voice sounded unnatural as I tried to show only a casual interest.

'Why—Heinrich Stelben,' he answered. 'If you are interested you shall see the cuttings from the newspapers. I keep them because so many of my guests are interested in our local celebrity.' The barman produced them immediately.

'May I borrow these?' I asked.

'But certainly. Only return them please. I wish to have them framed.'

I thanked him, confirmed our arrangement for going to the auction and hurried away to my room. I was greatly excited. Heinrich Stelben! Heinrich! I switched on the table light and took out the photograph Engles had given me. '*Für Heinrich, mein liebling—Carla*.' It was a common enough name. And yet it was strange. I picked up the cuttings. There were two of them and they both were from the *Corriere della Venezia*. They were quite short. Here they are in full, just as I translated them that first night in Cortina:

*Translated from the Corriere della Venezia of
November 20, 1946.*

CARABINIERI CAPTAIN CAPTURES GERMAN
WAR CRIMINAL IN HIDING NEAR CORTINA

Heinrich Stelben, German War Criminal, was captured
yesterday by Capitano Ferdinando Salvezza of the *Carabinieri*
in his hideout, the *rifugio* Col da Varda, near Cortina. He
was known in the district as Paulo Sordini. The Col da
Varda *rifugio* and *slittovia* were bought by him from the
collaborator, Alberto Oppo, one-time owner of the *Albergo
Excelsiore* in Cortina.

Heinrich Stelben was wanted for the murder of ten
British Commandos in the La Spezia area in 1944. He was
an officer of the hated *Gestapo* and he is also accused of
assisting in the deportation of Italians to Germany for
forced labour and of the murder of a number of Italian
political prisoners of the Left. He was also responsible for
transporting several consignments of gold from Italy to
Germany. The largest consignment was from the Banco
Commerciale del Popolo of Venice. Half of this consignment mysteriously disappeared before it reached Germany.
Stelben states that his troops mutinied and seized part of
the gold.

This is the second time that Heinrich Stelben has been
arrested by the *Carabinieri*. The first occasion was at a villa
on Lake Como shortly after the surrender of the German
Armies in Italy. He was taken to Milan and handed over
to the British for interrogation. A few days later he escaped.
He disappeared completely. Carla Rometta, a beautiful
cabaret dancer, with whom he had been associating, also
disappeared.

It is understood that his latest arrest was the result of

information lodged with the *Carabinieri*. With him, at the time of his arrest, were two Germans posing as Italian workmen. It is not known yet whether they are also war criminals.

Heinrich Stelben and his associates have been removed to Rome where they have been lodged in the Regina Coeli.

Translated from the Corriere della Venezia of
November 24, 1946.

GERMAN WAR CRIMINAL
COMMITS SUICIDE

Shortly after Heinrich Stelben, infamous German War Criminal, had been taken from the Regina Coeli and handed over to British Military Authorities, he committed suicide, according to a British press message. Whilst being interrogated, he broke a phial of prussic acid between his teeth.

The two Germans who had been arrested with him near Cortina were involved in the recent rioting in the Regina Coeli. It is understood that they were killed in the course of an attack on the *Carabinieri* by the inmates of the central block. It is not known whether they were wanted as war criminals.

I read those two cuttings through. And then I glanced again at the photograph. Carla! Carla Rometta! Heinrich Stelben! It was certainly a strange coincidence.

2

A 'Slittovia' is Auctioned

Joe Wesson looked tired and cross when I met him at breakfast the next morning. He had been up until the early hours playing stud poker with two Americans and a Czech. 'I'd like to get Engles out here,' he rumbled morosely. 'I'd like to put him on top of that damned col, cut the cable of the *slittovia* and leave him there. I'd like to give him such a bellyful of snow that he'd never even face ice in a drink again.'

'Don't forget he's a first-class ski-er,' I said, laughing. Engles had been in the British Olympic team at one time. 'He probably likes snow.'

'I know, I know. But that was in his early twenties, before the war. He's got soft since then. That's what the Army does for people. All he wants now is comfort—and liquor. You think he'd enjoy it up there in that hut—no women, no proper heating, nobody around to tell him how marvellous his ideas are—probably not even a bath?'

'Anyway, there's a bar,' I told him.

He gave a snort. 'Bar! I'm told that the man who runs that bar can trace congenital idiocy back through his family for three generations, that he specialises in *grappa* made from pure methylated spirits and, furthermore, that he is the dirtiest, laziest, stupidest Italian any one has ever met—and that's saying something. And here I'm supposed to drag my camera up to the top of that God-damned col and prance about in the snow taking pictures to satisfy Engles' megalomania. And I don't feel like going up a *slittovia* this morning. Those sort of things make me dizzy. It was constructed by the Germans and the man who owned it was arrested only a fortnight ago as a German war criminal. The cable is probably booby-trapped.'

I must admit that when I saw the thing, I didn't like it much myself. We stood at the bottom of it and looked up to the *rifugio* more than a thousand feet above us. Its gabled roofs and wooden belvedere were just visible at the top of the sleigh track cut through the pinewoods. It was perched high on the shoulder of Monte Cristallo, the great bastions of the mountain towering above it. It was about as remote from civilisation as an eagle's nest.

Our chauffeur got out of the car and shouted, 'Emilio!' A little man, wearing British battle-dress and the most enormous pair of snow boots, emerged from the concrete building that housed the cable plant. The boots dated back to the German occupation when there had been a flak position in the Tre Croci pass.

The snows had only just started down in Cortina, for it was early in the season yet. But up here it was already getting thick and the previous night's fall lay like a virgin blanket over everything.

We transferred our gear to the sleigh, putting our skis in the ski rack at the back. The black case of my typewriter and Joe Wesson's camera equipment seemed out of place. We climbed in. The man with the snow boots got up behind the steering wheel. He pulled over a switch and the cable tightened in front of us so that here and there it jerked clear of the snow. A soft crunching sound and we were gliding forward along the snow track. Almost immediately we were on the slope and the sleigh tilted upwards in an alarming fashion so that I found myself lying on my back rather than sitting on the seat. It was a peculiar and rather frightening sensation. We lost sight of the *rifugio*. We were looking up a long white avenue between the dark pines. It rose straight into the blue sky and was steep as the side of a house.

I looked back. Already the square Tre Croci Hotel was no bigger than a large black box resting on the white blanket of the pass. The road to Austria snaked through the pass like a dirty brown ribbon. The sun shone, but there was no sign of that 'sunny snow paradise' referred to in the tourist brochures. It was a lost and barren world of snow and black forest.

Ahead of us, the cable was strung taut like the string of a violin. There was no sound save the soft slither of the sleigh runs on the snow. The air was still between the dark pines. We were climbing at an angle of about sixty degrees. Joe leaned across me and spoke to the driver in English. 'Do these cables ever break on these things?' he asked.

The driver seemed to understand. He smiled and shook his head. '*Non, non, signore*. They have not never break. But the *funivia*—' that was the overhead cableway down at Cortina, and he let go the wheel for an instant and spread his hands in an expressive gesture. 'Once he break. Pocol *funivia*. *Molto pericoloso*.' And he grinned.

'What happened?' I asked.

'The cable, he gone. But the cable which draw him hold, so they fall twenty metres and do not touch earth. The passengers, they were much frightened.'

'Suppose this cable goes?' I enquired.

'It no go. It is a cable of the *tedesci*.' Then he crinkled the corners of his blue eyes. 'But if he do go—you see, *signori*, there is nothing that will not stop you.' And he pointed with a grin down the frightful track behind us.

'Thanks very much,' I said. And I was as glad as I have ever been to get out of that perilous vehicle at the *rifugio*.

It was large for a *rifugio*. Most of them only cater for the day visitor and have no sleeping accommodation. Col da Varda, however, had been designed to cater for those who come to the Dolomites for the ski-ing alone and who do not want to dance till the early hours.

It was timber-built of pines from the woods and had been constructed two years ago by the one-time owner of the Excelsiore.

It was built over and around the concrete housing of the cable machinery for the *slittovia*. With Teutonic thoroughness the Germans had placed the electrically operated haulage plant at the top of the sleigh track. The hut itself was a long building with great feet of pine piles driven deep into the snow. Its main feature was a large belvedere or platform, protected by glass like the bridge of a ship. It looked south and west across Tre Croci and down the pass to Cortina. The view was a magnificent study in black and white in the sunshine. And though it was still early and we were nearly 8,000 feet up, it was already warm enough to sit outside.

Back from the belvedere was a large eating room. It was lined with resined match-boarding and had big windows and long pine tables with forms on each side. In one corner was a typically Italian bar with a chromium-plated coffee geyser and, behind it, a shining array of bottles of all shapes in the midst of which swung the brass pendulum of a cuckoo clock. Between the bar and the door leading to the kitchen and the rest of the hut was a big tiled stove of Austrian pattern and there was an old upright piano in the far corner.

We went through the door towards the kitchen. Our first sight of Aldo was a head popped through the serving hatch in the kitchen door. It was a hairless head, sparsely garnished with a few grey tufts and both scalp and face gleamed as though freshly polished. The eyes had a dumb look and the mouth smiled vacantly as though apologising for the rest of it. The man was an ape. A moment's conversation with him convinced me of it. His smile was the only human thing about him. His brain was primordial. Joe Wesson said of him later that he was the sort of man who, if you told him to take away a plate and his hands were full of glasses, he would drop the glasses to pick up the plate. I asked him to show us to our rooms. He began to gobble at us confusedly like a turkey. His face became red. He gesticulated. Though his Italian was almost unintelligible, I gathered that he had received no booking. I told him to ring up the Splendido.

I had seen a telephone at the end of the bar. He shrugged his shoulders and said he had no room anyway.

'What's he gibbering about?' Joe asked. And when I told him, his cheeks began to quiver with anger. 'Nonsense,' he said. 'Tell the oaf to take his head out of that ridiculous hatch and come out here where my toe can get acquainted with the seat of his pants. I'd be delighted to have an excuse to go back to that nice comfortable hotel. But I'm damned if I go down that *slittovia* again. Once is quite enough for one day.'

I opened the door that framed Aldo's face and he came out, looking scared. I told him that my friend and I were getting angry. He began to gabble Italian at us again. 'Oh, to hell with it!' Joe exclaimed. 'Let's have a look at the rooms. There should be six and I was told only two were occupied.'

I nodded and we tramped up the uncarpeted stairs, Aldo following with a flood of Italian. At the top was a long corridor. The rooms were little match-board cubicles leading off it. The first door I opened revealed an empty room. I turned to Aldo. He spread his arms and drew down the corners of his mouth. The next door I opened showed a room with the bed unmade and clothes strewn around. The third room was actually occupied. Aldo had rushed to prevent my opening it, but Joe had swept him aside. A short, neat little man with long, sleek hair turning grey at the temples and a face that looked like a piece of dark crinkled rubber stood facing the door as I opened it. He was wildly over-dressed for a man living in the Col da Varda hut. He wore a natty near-dun-coloured suiting, a blue silk shirt and a yellow tie with red yachts sailing across it. He held a comb in his left hand and his attitude was curiously defensive. 'You are looking for me?' he asked in almost perfect English.

I hastened to explain. Aldo ducked beneath Joe's arm and became voluble. It was a duet in English and Italian. The occupant of the room cut Aldo short with a gesture of annoyance. 'My name is Stefan Valdini,' he said. 'This man is a fool,' he added, pointing to Aldo. 'He tries to save himself work by discouraging people from staying here. He is a lazy dog.' He had a soft purring voice that was a shade better than suave. '*Cretino!*' He flung the offensive term mildly at Aldo as though it were common usage. 'There are four rooms vacant. Give the English the two end ones.'

I had expected Aldo to become angry—you can call an Italian a bastard and give the crudest and most colourful description of his entire family and he will do no more than grin, but call him '*cretino*' and he usually becomes speechless with rage. But Aldo only grinned slavishly and said, '*Si, si, Signor Valdini—pronto.*'

So we found ourselves ushered into the two end cubicles. The window of Joe's room looked straight down the trackway of the *slittovia*. Mine, however, faced south across the belvedere. I could only see the *slittovia* by leaning out and getting the drips from the over-hanging snow down my neck. It was a grand view. The whole hillside of pines fell away, rank on rank of pointed tree-tops, to the valley. And to the right, above me, the great bastions of Monte Cristallo towered cold and forbidding even in the sunlight. 'Rum place, Neil.' Joe Wesson's bulk filled the narrow doorway. 'Who was the little man who looked like a pimp for a high-class *bordello*? Behaved as though he owned the place.'

'Don't know,' I said. I was busy unpacking my things and my mind was thinking what a place it was for the setting of a ski-ing film. 'Oldest inhabitant, perhaps—though he certainly looked as though he'd be more at home in a night club.'

'Well, now we're in we may as well have a drink to celebrate,' Joe muttered. 'I'll be at the bar. I'm going to try some of that red biddy they call *grappa*.'

The first sleigh-load of ski-ers arrived whilst I was still unpacking. They were a colourful crowd, sunburned and brightly clad. They thronged the belvedere, lounging in the warm sun, drinking out of tall glasses. They were talking happily in several languages. I watched them, fascinated, as in groups of two or three, or alone, they put on their skis and swooped out of sight down the slalom run to Tre Croci or disappeared into the dark firs, whooping 'Libera!' as they took the gentler track back to Cortina. Anna, a half-Italian, half-Austrian waitress, flirted in and out among the tables with trays laden with *salami* and eggs and *ravioli*. She had big laughing eyes and there was a quick smile and better service for the men who had no women with them. What a scene for technicolour! The colours stood out so startlingly against the black and white background.

The novelty of the setting was a spur to my determination to write something that Engles would accept. If I couldn't write a script here, I knew I should never be able to write one. I was still planning the script in my mind as I went down to join Joe at the bar.

At the bottom of the stairs, I came upon a tall, rather distinguished-looking man who was having a heated argument with Aldo. He had long, very thick-growing hair, strangely shot with grey. His face was deeply tanned, except where the white of a scar showed against the bulge of his jaw muscles. He was wearing an all-white ski suit with a yellow scarf round his neck. I realised what the trouble was immediately. 'Have you booked a room here?' I asked.

'Yes,' he said. 'This man is either a fool or he has given the room to somebody else and doesn't want to admit it.'

'I've just had the same trouble,' I said. 'I don't know why he doesn't want visitors. He just doesn't. But there are two rooms vacant at the moment. There's nobody in the one at the top of the stairs, so I should go up and stake your claim.'

'I will. Many thanks.' He gave me a lazy smile and took his things up the stairs. Aldo gave a shrug and dropped the corners of his mouth. Then he followed on.

Joe and I spent the remainder of the morning sitting out in the sunshine drinking cognac and discussing the shots Engles would expect. The multi-coloured plumage of the ski-ers and the babel of tongues that ranged from the tinselled guttural of Austrian to the liquid flood of Italian was a background to our conversation; absorbed, but not remarked in detail. Joe was no longer disgruntled at being perched up here on the cold shoulder of an Alp. He was a cameraman now, interested only in angles and lights and setting. He was an artist who has been given a good subject. And I was doubly preoccupied—I was listening to Joe and at the same time rolling an idea for a script round my mind.

I did not notice her arrive. I don't know how long she had been there. I just glanced up suddenly and saw her. Her head and shoulders stood out against the white back-cloth of a snow-draped fir. For a second I was puzzled. I thought I knew her and yet I could not place her. Then, as I stared, she took off her dark glasses and looked straight at me, dangling them languidly between long slender brown fingers. And then I remembered and dived for my wallet and the photograph Engles had given me.

The likeness was striking. But I wasn't sure. The photograph was old and faded, and the girl who had signed herself 'Carla' had shorter, sleeked-back hair. But the features looked the same. I glanced up again at the woman seated at the table on the other side of the belvedere. Her raven-black hair swept up in a great wave above her high forehead and tumbled in a mass to her shoulders. The way she sat and her every movement proclaimed an almost animal consciousness of her body. She wasn't particularly young, nor was she particularly beautiful. Her mouth, scarlet to match her ski suit, was too wide and full, and there were deep lines at the corners of her eyes. But she was exciting. She was all of a man's baser thoughts come true. She caught my eye as I compared her with the photograph in my hand. Her glance was an idle caress, speculative and not disinterested, like the gaze of an animal that is bored and is looking for someone to play with.

'My God, Neil!' Joe tapped me on the arm. 'Are you trying to bed that woman down?'

'Don't be revolting,' I said. I felt slightly embarrassed. Joe was so solidly British in that foreign set-up. 'Why make a vulgar suggestion like that on a lovely morning?'

'You were looking at her as though you wanted to eat her,' he replied. 'She's got that little Valdini chap for boy-friend. You want to go steady with these people. Knives, you know. They're not civilised. He struck me as an ugly little fellow to start an argument with over a girl.' He was right. The man sitting opposite her was Valdini. He had his back towards us.

'Don't be absurd, Joe,' I said. Then I showed him the photograph, keeping my thumb across the writing. 'Is that the same girl?' I asked him.

He cocked his head on one side and screwed up his little bloodshot eyes. 'Hmm. Could be. How did you get hold of that?'

'It's the picture of an Italian actress,' I lied quickly. 'I knew her in Naples just before Anzio. She gave it to me then. The point is—is the woman sitting over there the girl I knew or not?'

'I don't know,' he replied. 'And frankly, old man, I don't give a damn. But it seems to me that the best way to find out is to go and ask her.'

Joe, of course, did not realise the difficulty. Engles had said, do nothing. But I had to be certain. It seemed so fantastic that she should turn up on the very first day I was at Col da Varda. But the likeness was certainly striking. I suddenly made up my mind and got to my feet. 'You're right,' I said. 'I'll go and find out.'

'Well, don't go treading on the corns of that over-dressed little pimp. I'm a good chucker-out in a London bar. But I'm too big a target to play around with people I suspect of being expert knife-throwers.'

She had seen me get up and her eyes watched me intently as I crossed the belvedere. Valdini looked up as I reached the table. 'Excuse me,' I said to her, 'but I feel sure I met you when I was in Italy with the British Army.'

There was an awkward pause. She was watching me. So was Valdini. Then she gave me a sudden warm smile. 'I do not think so,' she said in English. Her voice was deep and liquid. It was like a purr. 'But you look nice. Come and sit down and tell me about it.'

Valdini, who had been watching me guardedly, now sprang to his feet. Polished and suave, he produced a chair for me from the next table.

'Well,' she said as I sat down, 'where was it that we met?'

I hesitated. Her eyes were very dark and they were looking at me with open amusement. 'I think your name is Carla,' I said.

The eyes suddenly went blank. They were cold and hard— hard like the eyes in the photograph.

'I think you have made a mistake,' she said coldly.

Valdini came to the rescue. 'Perhaps I should make an intro-duction. This is the Contessa Forelli. And this is Mr Blair. He is from an English film company.' I wondered how he had found that out and why he had taken the trouble.

'I am sorry,' I said. 'I thought your surname might be—Rometta.'

I was convinced she caught her breath. But her eyes did not change. She had control of herself. 'Well, now perhaps you know you have made a mistake, Mr Blair,' she said.

I was still not sure. I pulled the photograph out of my pocket and showed it to her. 'Surely this is a photograph of you?' I said. I kept the bottom part covered.

She leaned forward quickly. 'Where did you get that?' There was nothing purrful about her voice as she shot the question at me. It was hard and angry and brittle. Then, with an abrupt change of tone, she said, 'No, you can see for yourself that it is not my photograph. But it is strange. It is a great likeness. Let me look at it.' And she extended a strong brown hand imperiously.

I pretended not to hear her request. I put the photograph back in my pocket. 'Most extraordinary!' I murmured. 'The like-ness is quite remarkable. I felt certain—' I rose to my feet. 'You must excuse me Contessa,' I said, bowing. 'The likeness is quite extraordinary.'

'Don't go, Mr Blair.' She gave me a hard, brilliant smile and the purr was back in her voice. 'Stay and have a drink—and tell me more about that photograph. It is so nearly myself that I would like to know more about it. I am intrigued. Stefan, order a drink for Mr Blair.'

'No, please, Contessa,' I said. 'I have been guilty of sufficient bad manners for one day. Please accept my apologies. It was the likeness—I had to be certain.'

I went back to Joe. 'Well,' he said, as I resumed my seat, 'was she the girl or not?'

'I think so,' I told him.

'Couldn't you make certain?'

'She didn't want to be recognised,' I explained.

'I don't blame her,' he grunted. 'I wouldn't want to be recognised in the company of that little tyke, especially if I were a woman. Look at him getting up now. He positively bounces with his own self-importance.'

I watched the Contessa rise and put on her skis. She did not once glance in my direction. The incident might never have happened. She took the dapper little Valdini out on to the snow for a moment's conversation. Then, with a flash of her sticks, she swooped out of sight down the slalom run to Tre Croci. As he came back, Valdini darted a quick glance at me.

We had lunch out on the belvedere and, afterwards, Joe went out with his camera and a pair of borrowed snow-shoes and I retired to my room to start work on the script. But I could not settle down. I could not concentrate. My mind kept wandering to the mystery of Engles' interest in Col da Varda. First the story of Heinrich Stelben's arrest. Now the Contessa Forelli, who looked so like Carla. It was stretching coincidence too far to believe that there was no connection. And what was it about the place that drew them here? If only Engles had told me more. But perhaps he hadn't known much more. The *slittovia* was beginning to dominate my thoughts as it dominated the *rifugio*.

I could hear it even up in my bedroom, a low, grating drone whenever the sleigh came up or went down. And in the bar, which was right over the concrete machine room, the sound of it was almost deafening.

At length I gave up any attempt to write. I tapped out a report for Engles and went down to the bar in time to see Joe returning with his camera. The snow-shoes were circular contraptions fixed to his boots. He looked like a great clumsy elephant as he floundered up the slope of the Cortina run. The day visitors had all left long ago and it was getting dark and very cold outside. The *rifugio* seemed shrinking into itself for the night. Aldo stoked up the great tiled stove and we gravitated naturally to the bar and *anisetto*.

It was whilst we were standing round the bar that an incident occurred that is worth recording. It was a small thing—or appeared so at the time—yet it was very definitely a part of the pattern of events. There were four of us there at the time—Joe Wesson and myself, Valdini and the new arrival, who had introduced himself as Gilbert Mayne. He was Irish, but by his conversation appeared to have seen a good deal of the world, particularly the States.

Valdini had been trying to pump me about that photograph. It was difficult to put him off. He was what schoolboys would call 'bumptious.' You hit him and he bounced. He had a hide like a brontosaurus. But in the end I managed to convince him that I regarded the matter as being of little importance and that I really felt that I had made a foolish mistake. The talk gradually drifted to strange means of conveyance, such as the *slittovia*. Mayne, I remember, was talking about riding the tubs on overhead haulage gear, when the cable machinery began to drone under our feet. The steady grinding sound of it made conversation almost impossible. The whole room seemed to shake. 'Who'd be coming up as late as this?' Mayne asked.

Valdini looked up from cleaning his nails with a match-stick.

'That will be the other visitor here. He is a Greek. His name is Keramikos. Why he stays here I do not know. I think he likes Cortina better.' He grinned and, transferring the match-stick to his mouth, began to pick his teeth. 'He is of the Left. He knows all that transpires politically in Greece. And he likes the women. The Contessa, for instance—he cannot take his eyes off her. He gloats, as you would say.' And he sucked his teeth obscenely.

The sound of the *slittovia* slowed and ceased. Valdini kept on talking. 'He reminds me of a Greek business man I once knew,' he continued. 'I was running a boat on the Nile. It was beautiful and very profitable. For tired business men, you know. The gairls were all hand-picked.' The way he said 'gairls' made it sound like a breed of animals. 'It was a sort of show boat.'

'You mean a floating brothel,' Joe grunted. 'Why the hell don't you call things by their proper names? Anyway, I don't find the subject a particularly pleasing one. I'm not interested in your brothels.'

'But, Mistair Wesson, it is so sordid the way you talk about it. It was beautiful, you understand. There was the moonlight. The moon is lovely on the Nile. And there was the music. It was a very good business. And this Greek—I forget his name—he was a wealthy business man from Alexandria—always he wanted a different gairl. He was a gold mine. I made a great deal—' He stopped then because he realised that we were not listening.

Whilst he had been talking brisk steps had sounded on the boarding of the belvedere. Then the door had opened and the cold dark of the outside world had invaded the warm room. I suppose we had all been watching the door with some interest. One is always interested in getting the first glimpse of a person one is expected to live with in an isolated place. It was mere idle curiosity.

But the man who entered stopped in the doorway at the sight of the four of us grouped about the bar. He seemed rooted to the spot, his thick-set body framed in the dark gap like a statue in its niche. He was looking at Mayne. And Mayne had stiffened. His tall figure was tensed. It was only for a second. And during that second the atmosphere was electric. Then Mayne turned to the bar and ordered another round of drinks. The Greek closed the door and came over to the bar. Everything was suddenly normal again.

I was convinced Mayne and the Greek had recognised each other. But there was no indication of this as the Greek came over to us and introduced himself. He was stockily built with a round face and blue eyes that peered short-sightedly through thick-lensed, rimless glasses. His light brown hair was very thin on top and his neck was short, so that his head seemed to be set straight into the wide powerful shoulders.

He spoke good English in a low, rather thick voice. He had a way of thrusting his head forward when making a point, a mannerism which gave him a somewhat belligerent air.

Only once throughout the evening did anything occur to support my theory that he and Mayne had met before. We were discussing the revolt of the Greek Brigade in Egypt during the war. Keramikos was extremely well informed on the details of it. So well informed, in fact, that Joe suddenly emerged from a prolonged silence and said quietly, 'You talk as though you organised the whole damned thing.' I could have sworn the Greek exchanged a quick glance with Mayne. It was not a friendly glance. It was as though on that point they were on common ground.

One other thing occurred that night that seemed strange to me. Engles had wanted full information on the people staying at Col da Varda, so I decided to send him a photograph of them. After dinner, I persuaded Joe to get his Leica and take a few shots of the group at the bar. I told him I wanted the shots to prove to Engles that the hut would have more atmosphere than a hotel for the indoor scenes. Little Valdini was delighted when Joe came in with his camera and began posing immediately. But when Mayne and Keramikos saw it, they turned their backs and began talking earnestly. Joe asked them to face the camera and Mayne said over his shoulder, 'We're not part of your film company, you know.'

Joe grunted and took a few pictures. But only Valdini and Aldo were facing the camera. I began to ask him questions about the camera. I knew perfectly well how it worked, but I was determined to get a picture of those two. He let me handle it and I took it over to the bar under the light. The cuckoo suddenly sprang out of the clock. 'Cuckoo! Cuckoo!' Mayne and Keramikos looked up, startled, and I snapped them.

At the click of the camera, Mayne turned to me. 'Did you take a photograph?' he asked, and there was a note of anger in his voice.

'I'm not sure,' I said. 'Why?'

He looked at me hard. He had cold, light-coloured eyes.

'He does not like being photographed,' Valdini said, and there was malice in his tone.

Mayne's eyes hardened with anger. But he said nothing to Valdini and turned back with a casual air to continue his conversation with Keramikos.

These are small things, but they stood out like wrong notes in a smoothly played piece of music. I had a strange feeling that all these people—Valdini, Keramikos and Mayne—were suppressing violent antipathy beneath a casual exterior.

Shortly after breakfast the next morning I left for Cortina. Mayne came with me. I had mentioned the auction to him the previous night and he had expressed a desire to come. As we were leaving, we passed Joe cursing a pair of skis on to his feet. 'Feel like a pair of canoes,' he grumbled. 'Six years since I did this. Doubt if my blood pressure will stand it. If I break my neck, I'll sue Engles for it. But I can't get the pictures I want otherwise.' He had a small movie camera slung round his neck. 'If I'm not back by tea-time, Neil, you'd better call out the bloodhounds. Where are you off to?'

When I told him, he gave me an old-fashioned look. 'Far be it from me to come between you and what you apparently regard as amusement, old man,' he said. 'But Engles is expecting a script out of you. And he detests slow workers.' He shrugged his shoulders. 'Oh, well, you know the man. But maybe he was less exacting in the Army. With a film unit, he just isn't human. Why do you think I'm putting on these damned things?'

I thanked him, for he meant it kindly. He wasn't to know that Engles had already got a script.

It was a glorious morning. The sky was blue. The sun shone. But the world was deathly still. No birds sang in the dark fir woods. In all that glistening country there was no sign of life. The *slittovia* was even more terrifying going down. We sat facing the *rifugio*—or rather we lay on our backs facing it. And we travelled down through the lane between the firs backwards. As though by mutual consent we talked. And the talk developed into a comparison of the merits of various Italian composers. Mayne knew his opera and hummed snatches to illustrate his points. He preferred the gay swiftness of *The Barber* and the subtle comedy of lesser known operas, like *I Quatri Rustici*, to the heavier pieces. In this we differed, for *Traviata* is my favourite. But we were on common ground in our enthusiasm for the spectacle of *Aida*, played beneath a full moon in the open-air theatre in Rome with the colossal, shadowy bulk of the Baths of Caracalla as its setting. I must confess that, at that moment, I liked his company immensely.

As we came into Cortina by car, the streets were full of ski-ers moving out to the various runs. They were a gaily coloured throng, their tanned faces glowing with the cold mountain air. The little town, with its gables and high, pencil-sharp church steeple, looked bright and gay in the sunlight. There were tourists wandering the snow-piled pavements, gazing in the shop windows or sitting in steamy-windowed cafés drinking coffee and cognac. The two overhead cable railways—the *funivias*—stretched out their cables, like antennae, on either side of the town. The one to the left climbed to Mandres in one cable jump and then scaled the heights of Faloria in a single sweep. It was just possible to make out the line of the cable, like a frail thread, and the little red car against the sun-warmed brown of the Faloria cliffs. On the other side of the town, a shorter cable made one bound to the rounded knoll of Pocol, with its hotels and the *slittovias* leading to the more advanced runs—Col Druscie and the Tofana Olympic run.

I left Mayne at the Luna and then went on to the *officio della posta* where I caught the air mail with my second report to Engles and the roll of film. When I arrived at the Splendido, Mancini was drinking in the bar with several fellow hoteliers. He greeted me as though I were the one person he had been waiting for. He had great ability as a host. 'You must have a drink, Mr Blair,' he said. 'The Luna is always so cold.' And he grinned like a playful lion at a thin, neat little Italian, whom I guessed to be the owner of the Gran' Albergo Luna. 'A large Martini—yes? It will prevent *ennui*. Then we will go and buy the *slittovia*. Afterwards we will celebrate. Whenever one of us buys something, we all celebrate. It is the excuse. Always there must be the excuse.'

The lounge of the Luna was warm and cosy when we arrived. There were between twenty and thirty people there—all men and mostly Italian. They had the indifference of spectators. They were not there to buy. They were there because it was a social function and there would be drinks afterwards. They crowded round Mancini, laughing and chattering, congratulating him on his latest acquisition. Mayne was sunk in an easy-chair with a tall glass in front of him. I went across and joined him. He pulled up a chair and ordered me a drink. But he did not seem interested in conversation. He was watching the scene closely. His interest switched suddenly to the door. I followed the direction of his gaze and was surprised to see that Valdini had entered. He moved jauntily with an air of colossal self-importance. This morning it was a darker suiting with a sheen of mauve in it. The shirt was cream-coloured and the tie red, shot with blue flashes of forked lightning. 'What's Valdini doing here?' I asked. 'Shouldn't have thought he would have been interested in an auction.'

'I don't know.' Mayne spoke softly, as though to himself, and there was a puzzled frown on his dark handsome face.

Then the auctioneer entered. He moved with the self-conscious air of a man about to conjure something out of a hat. You felt there should have been a fanfare of trumpets to herald that entrance. He moved through the room as though it were an audience, bowing to acquaintances, pausing a moment here and there to shake a hand. You felt it was his moment. He had two waiters hovering behind him. He indicated a table. He had it moved. He chose a chair. It was placed ready for him. He tossed his papers on to the table. The maitre d'hotel brought on his hammer and set it carefully on the polished table top. An imaginary fleck of dust was hastily removed. Then finally, the auctioneer settled himself behind the table. He beat upon the top of it dramatically. The room began to settle itself. Mancini moved to a vacant table just near me. The pack followed at his heels. He pulled his chair next to me. 'He is amusing—yes?' he said, nodding towards the auctioneer.

'The entrance was nicely handled,' I said.

He smiled and nodded. 'We are a theatrical race,' he said. 'That is why, when an Italian is executed, he dies well. He may not like the result, but he enjoys the moment. Now, you will see. We shall be very quiet and he will talk for a long time. We know this *slittovia* as well as we know our own hotels. But he will describe it to us as though we had never seen it. He will make the lyric of the description. He will become excited. He will make gestures. It will be the grand performance. And then, when he is exhausted, I shall make the bid and it will be sold for what has already been arranged. It is all very un-English,' he added with a sly twinkle. 'But I am glad you are amused. If you were not amused, you would be bored, and that would make me sad.'

The hammer crashed on to the table top again. The room stopped talking. The curtain had been rung up. The performance had begun. The auctioneer began reading the conditions of sale. He slipped through it rapidly. It gave him no scope. But then came the reasons for the sale. He told of its original purchase by the 'miserable' Sordini from the collaborator who had once owned the Excelsiore. He told of Sordini's arrest, of the 'world-shaking' news that he was Heinrich Stelben, a German war criminal wanted for the most 'terrible, fearful and blood-thirsty crimes against the Italian and British peoples.' He drew a word portrait of this 'madman.' He touched briefly on the crimes of the 'terrible *tedesci*,' and barely saved himself from a short history of how the Italian people had been 'roused by terrible and barbaric acts' and had forced the 'hated' Germans to surrender. Then suddenly, *pianissimo*, he began to describe the *slittovia* and the hut on Col da Varda. Gradually he whipped himself into a lyrical frenzy—it was a 'stupendous' opportunity for an astute business man with 'grand' ideas, an incredibly beautiful property, thoroughly equipped by 'brilliant German engineers,' a 'small hotel with finer panoramic views than the Eagle's Nest at Berchtesgaden.'

Then suddenly his voice ceased. The room was silent as though the performance had taken everyone's breath away. At any moment I expected a wild outburst of applause. Surely they must demand an *encore*. But the room remained silent. The auctioneer ran his fingers through his long hair, which had fallen in dank strands across his face. His thin features wore a disappointed look. He pushed his glasses farther back on his long nose and offered the property for sale in a cold matter-of-fact voice.

'*Due centi cinquanta mille.*' Mancini's voice was quiet and there was a tired air of finality about the offer. A quarter of a million *lire.* The auctioneer pretended to be aggrieved. That was the low reserve placed on the property by the Government. Mancini had doubtless put in some hard social work to get the figure down as low as that. The auctioneer called for further bids. But he knew it was hopeless. He knew it was all arranged. His brief moment was over. He was no longer interested. He gave a shrug and raised his hammer.

'*Tre centi mille.*' The voice was quiet and smooth. A sudden flood of surprised volubility swept the room. Heads were turned, necks craned. I knew the voice before I picked out his neat little figure strategically placed where the sunlight fell on him in a shaft from one of the tall windows. It was Valdini. His chest, gaily coloured like the plumage of some elaborate tropical fowl, was puffed out importantly. His dark rubbery face beamed as he held the limelight.

Mancini was talking rapidly to the men around him. He was literally quivering with anger. I turned to Mayne to make some comment. But he did not appear to hear me. He was leaning forward, gazing at Valdini with intense interest. He was smiling slightly and there was a glint in his eyes—of amusement or excitement, I could not tell which.

The auctioneer was clearly astonished. He asked Valdini if he had heard correctly. Valdini repeated his bid—three hundred thousand *lire*. All eyes were turned to Mancini, to see what the great man would do. He had recovered himself. One of his friends slipped quietly out of the room. Mancini lit a cigarette, settled himself more comfortably in his chair and raised the bidding ten thousand.

Valdini did not hesitate. He went straight up to four hundred thousand. 'And ten,' said Mancini. 'Fifty,' came from the window. Mancini raised to sixty. Valdini jumped to five hundred thousand. So it went on, Mancini going up in tens and Valdini in fifties till they hit the million. Word of the duel had spread quickly through the hotel. People were standing thick about the door.

At a million *lire* there was a pause in the bidding. Mancini had been getting slower and slower in his bids as the figures rose. He sat hunched in his seat, his jaw set and his eyes sullen. It was not the money he cared about so much as this deliberate flouting of his position in Cortina. It hurt his pride to have to haggle in public for something that everyone knew he had arranged in private. I leaned across to him and ventured to ask him what the property was worth. 'To me, perhaps a million,' he replied. 'To an outsider, nothing.'

'You mean you will boycott the place and Valdini will lose his money?' I asked.

'Valdini?' He laughed mirthlessly. 'Valdini is a dirty little Sicilian gangster. He loses nothing. It is not his money.'

'He is acting for someone then?' I asked.

He nodded. 'The Contessa Forelli, I think. I have sent someone to try and find out.'

The auctioneer had grown tired of waiting. He poised his hammer. Mancini raised the bidding ten again.

'*Cinquanta*' came the monotonous voice of Valdini.

'*Sessanta.*'

'*Cento.*'

'I do not understand it,' Mancini muttered angrily to me. 'They will pay through the nose and make a bad business of it. There are hidden reasons. That Forelli woman is up to something. She is too clever with men.'

The man who had slipped out for Mancini returned and whispered in his ear. '*Ma, perche?*' I heard him ask. The man shrugged his shoulders. Mancini turned and raised the bidding again. 'It is Forelli,' he said to me. 'But why I do not know. She must have a reason. If I knew it and it was worth the money, I would give her a defeat. But I do not throw money in the drain, you understand.' He was near the limit he would go. I felt sorry for him. He did not want me to think him unsporting or lacking in courage. He did not like an Englishman to see him defeated.

The bidding crawled slowly up to the one and a half million mark. Then Valdini astonished the whole room by changing his tactics. He jumped from one and a half to two millions. There was a note of triumph in his voice. He guessed the hotelier would not follow him to that figure.

His psychology was right. Mancini shrugged his shoulders as the auctioneer glanced at him enquiringly. Then he rose to his feet. The bidding was over. Mancini was making a grand exit as though washing his hands of a preposterous business. The auctioneer raised his hammer. This time his movement was quicker.

But as the hammer rose, a sharp firm voice said, '*Due e mezzo.*'

The room gasped. Two and a half million *lire*!

Mancini sat down again, searching the room. For a moment there was not a sound. I looked across at Valdini. The beaming importance had been wiped from his face by this fresh bid. His features had a mean look. The auctioneer searched out and found the new bidder. He was a small, pallid man in a dark grey suit seated uncomfortably on an upright chair. He looked like an undertaker. His clothes did not suggest that he was worth a lot of money. Asked to repeat his bid, he did so in the same firm voice.

The auctioneer glanced at Valdini who nodded his head with a worried look and raised the bidding a hundred thousand. '*Tre millioni.*' The voice was firm and impersonal. It hushed the sudden outburst of excited conversation.

'This is incredible,' I said to Mayne.

His eyes were fixed intently on the new bidder. He did not hear me. I turned to Mancini. 'Who is the little man who is bidding?' I asked him.

'A lawyer from Venezia,' he said. 'He is a partner in a firm which works for big industrial enterprises. He, too, is bidding for a client.' His tone showed his concern. I think he was envisaging a big syndicate invading Cortina with money enough to put himself and his friends out of business.

Valdini suddenly jumped five hundred thousand. His voice was pitched a shade high as he made the bid. It was a violent gesture. 'Shock tactics,' I whispered to Mayne.

He was still watching the scene intently, his eyes narrowed. I noticed the knuckles of his hands were white where they gripped the chair. He was clearly very excited by the bidding. Suddenly he relaxed. 'What?—oh, shock tactics—yes. Valdini is near his limit.' And he turned away again, tense and watchful.

The little lawyer seemed to hesitate. He was watching Valdini closely. Valdini was nervous. His eyes darted here and there round the room. Everyone was watching him. Everyone sensed that he was approaching his limit. A gust of excited whisperings filled the room. The cold voice of the lawyer stilled it. Four million and one hundred thousand, he bid.

The room gasped. The lawyer was reckoning on Valdini's limit being four million. One glance at Valdini's face showed that he was right. The bidding had passed beyond him. Valdini asked permission of the auctioneer to telephone his client. Permission was refused. He pleaded. His client, he explained, had not expected the bidding to go so high. He suggested that the auctioneer himself had not expected it. It was fantastic. In such exceptional circumstances the auctioneer should permit him to refer to his client for instructions. The auctioneer refused.

He and the room waited in suspense, watching the workings of Valdini's mind. It was clear that he wanted to go on, but that he did not dare without further instructions. The hammer rose, hesitated as the auctioneer raised his eyebrows in Valdini's direction, and then finally fell.

The astonishing auction was over. The *slittovia* was sold to an unknown buyer.

3

Murder for Two

There was no celebration after the auction. The room split up into excited, gesticulating groups. Mancini went off to confer with half the hoteliers in Cortina. I don't know where Mayne went to—he just seemed to drift off on his own. I found myself having a lonely lunch at the Luna, trying to figure out what all this had to do with Engles.

When I got back to Col da Varda, there were several parties of ski-ers there, for the sun was still warm. I went straight up to my room and wrote out a report of the auction for Engles. By the time I went downstairs again the ski-ers had all gone. But Valdini was there. He was standing at the bar, drinking. He had a furtive look.

'You had bad luck,' I said for the sake of something to say.

He shrugged his shoulders. He would like to have appeared unconcerned. But he was very drunk. He could not control his features. He looked so wretchedly miserable that I felt almost sorry for the little bounder. 'Anyway, you had Mancini licked,' I encouraged him.

'Mancini,' he snarled. 'He is a fool. He knows nothing. But that other . . .' He suddenly burst into tears. It was a disgusting sight.

'I am sorry,' I said. I think my voice must have sounded rather stiff.

'Sorry!' he snarled with a sudden change of mood. 'Why should you be sorry? It is me—Stefan—who is sorry. I should be the proprietor here now. This place should be mine.' He made

45

a grand wavering movement of his arm, and then added, 'Yes, mine—and everything in it.' And he peered forward at me cunningly.

'You mean it should belong to the Contessa Forelli, don't you?' I said.

His eyes focused on me soberly for a second. 'You know too much, Blair,' he said. 'You know too damn much.' He seemed to be turning something over in his mind. His expression was not a pleasant one. I remembered Mancini's description of him—'a dirty little Sicilian gangster.' I had thought at the time that Mancini was just giving vent to his anger. But it occurred to me now that perhaps that was just what Valdini was. He looked ugly, and dangerous.

Footsteps sounded on the wooden boards of the belvedere and the door was thrown open. It was the Contessa, and she was in a blazing temper—it showed in her face and in her eyes and in the way she moved. She was all in white—white ski suit, white gloves, white tam-o'-shanter. Only her scarf and ski socks were red. She looked hard at Valdini. The little man seemed to curl up, deflated. Then she looked past me to the bar. 'Aldo!' she called.

The ape came running. She ordered cognac and went out to a table in the sun.

'I think your boss wants you,' I said to Valdini.

He glared at me. But he made no retort and followed Aldo and the cognac out on to the belvedere. When Aldo returned, he went behind the bar and produced a cable envelope. 'For you, *signore*,' he said, handing it across to me.

'When did this come?' I asked him in Italian.

'This morning, *signore*. Just before you left. Emilio brought it up when he came to fetch you this morning.'

'Then why the hell didn't you give it to me?' I asked angrily. 'Can't you see it's a cable and therefore important?' He smiled sheepishly and spread his hands in the inevitable gesture that he used to explain all his shortcomings.

I ripped open the envelope. It was from Engles and read: *Presume attending auction. Cable fullest report Mancini unbuy. Engles.*

I folded the cable and put it in my pocket. He wanted a cabled report if Mancini was not the buyer. Had he expected there to be an unknown buyer at the auction? What difference could it make to him who bought Col da Varda? However, he wanted the information by cable and that meant going down to Cortina again. I decided to give myself a try-out on skis. I hadn't done any ski-ing since I had gone up to Tolmina from Rome, and that had been two years ago. I was just going to get my ski things when I remembered a question that I wanted to put to Aldo. It had been in my mind ever since Valdini had begun to bid at the auction.

'You remember you did not want to let us have rooms here?' I said to him in Italian. 'That was because Signor Valdini had instructed you to turn visitors away, wasn't it?'

He looked helplessly towards the belvedere. He was afraid to answer. But it was clear that I was right. '*Non importante,*' I said. It looked as though Valdini and the Contessa had planned to close the place down as soon as the purchase had been completed. Why?

I went up to my room and got my things. I typed out my reply to Engles' cable. It read: *Auction sensation. Sold unknown purchaser operating Venice lawyer. Valdini for Carla outbid Mancini two million. Unknown outbid Valdini four million. Blair.*

When I got downstairs again the Contessa was alone in the bar. As I made for the door, she suddenly called out, 'Mr Blair!'

I turned. She was leaning against the bar. Her eyes were inviting and her wide mouth was made attractive by a little smile that lifted the corners of it. 'Come and have a drink with me,' she suggested. 'I do not like drinking by myself. Besides, I wish to talk to you. I would like to know more about my photograph.'

I felt ill-at-ease. She was hard and hard women frighten me. Besides, how was I to explain how that photograph came into my possession? 'I'm sorry,' I said, 'but I have to go down to Cortina.' My voice sounded cold and unfriendly.

The corners of her mouth drooped in mock disappointment and there was a hint of laughter in her dark eyes. She knocked back her drink and came towards me. Her ski boots made hardly a sound on the bare boards. She could have danced in them. 'You shall not escape me so easily,' she said, and with a ripple of laughter, she tucked her slim brown hand under my arm. 'I too must go back to Cortina. You will not refuse to escort me?' She did not wait for an answer, but exclaimed, 'Oh—why are you English so stiff? You do not laugh. You are not gay. You are afraid of women. You are so reserved and so damned dignified.' She laughed. 'But you are nice. You have—how shall I say?—an air. And it is nice, your air. Now, you will escort me to Cortina— yes?' She had her head cocked on one side and there was an impish gleam in her eyes that was quite disturbing. 'Please do not look so serious, Mr Blair. I will not seduce you on the way down.' She sighed. 'Once—yes. But now—one gets old, you know.' She shrugged her shoulders and walked across to her skis.

'I am afraid it will be a question of you escorting me, Contessa,' I apologised as I fixed my skis. 'It is two years since I did any ski-ing.'

'Do not worry,' she said. 'It will come back. And Cortina is not a difficult run. You need to do a lot of stemming on the first part. After that it is a straight run. Are you ready?' She was standing poised on the slope that led into the fir woods.

My feet felt very clumsy. I remembered what Joe had said that morning about his skis feeling like a couple of canoes. That is just what mine felt like. I wished I had not told her that I was going into Cortina. 'Yes, I'm ready,' I said, and slithered across the belvedere to the start of the run.

She laid a slim, white-gloved hand on my arm. Her mood changed. 'I think we are going to become good friends,' she said. 'I shall call you Neil. It is such a nice name. And you had better call me—Carla.' She gave me a quick glance to see that the point had registered and then, with a smile and a flash of sticks, she plunged down into the dark firs. Whilst I was still hesitating on the brink of the run, her cry of 'libera!' floated back to me from the woods, telling me that already she had reached the point where the ski track from Monte Cristallo joins the Col da Varda—Cortina run.

I thrust myself forward with my sticks, saw my ski points tilt on to the slope and then I was hurtling through the cold air, my skis biting deeply on the frozen surface of the run. I took it slowly, snow-ploughing on the steeper slopes so that my ankles ached and stemming hard on the bends. The track was not really steep. But to my unaccustomed skis, it seemed precipitous as it wound down through the black straight trunks of the firs. I had no time to think about the Contessa's reason for that sudden admission of identity. Brain and muscle were alike concentrated on getting down the run.

Halfway down to the road I found the Contessa waiting for me in a patch of sunlight. She looked a ghostly figure in her white ski suit, which was cream-coloured against the purer white of the snow. I nerved myself for a half-Christi and it came off. I stopped dead beside her in a flurry of ice-crisp snow. A little wobbly it was true, but still I had done it and it takes quite a bit of nerve to try it, if you haven't been on skis for a long time and aren't particularly good anyway.

'Bravo!' she applauded. She had a cigarette in her mouth and was holding the packet out to me.

I took one. I was feeling very pleased with myself. I had been trying to show off and her quietly voiced 'bravo!' gave me immense satisfaction. My hand was trembling with the nervous excitement of the effort as I lit her cigarette.

There was a short silence between us. It was not an embar-rassed silence. It was more the silence of two people thinking out what line they are going to take. It was very quiet in the woods and the sun was warm. My body glowed and tingled. The cigarette was Turkish and the scent of it was an exotic intrusion in that solitude of snow and fir. My brain was working fast. I knew what she was going to ask. That was why she had stopped for a smoke. And I had to think of some natural explanation of how I had come by that photograph. How had Engles got hold of it? I glanced at her. She was watching me covertly through a veil of smoke. She was expecting me to say something. I nerved myself to break the silence between us. 'So that *was* your photograph?' I said, hoping that my voice did not sound nervous.

She drew deeply at her cigarette. 'Yes,' she said and her voice was pitched strangely low. 'You were quite right. I was once called Carla Rometta.' She hesitated then. I waited and at length she said, 'You seem to know more about my affairs than I like in a stranger. For we have not met before, you know.'

'No,' I said. 'We have not met before.'

'You lied to me.'

'I had to open the conversation somehow.'

'So, we have not met. Yet you have my photograph. That picture was taken—oh, a long time ago, in Berlin.'

'Yes,' I said. 'It was taken by a Berlin photographer.'

'May I see it please?'

'I have not got it on me,' I lied.

She gave me a quick, searching glance. 'I see,' she said. 'I find it strange that you should carry my photograph when we have not met before. You will explain to me the reason—yes?' She was watching me. I concentrated on my cigarette. 'I had signed it?' she asked. 'And written on it also?'

I nodded.

'What had I written—please tell me.' There was a tremor in her voice.

'It was to Heinrich,' I told her.

A sigh escaped her lips and she was silent for a moment. Then she said, 'You seem to know much of my affairs. Stefan tells me that you were at the auction this morning and that you know he was trying to buy Col da Varda on my behalf. How did you know that?'

'Edouardo Mancini told me,' I replied.

'That ugly old pig!' She gave a short laugh. 'Nothing can happen in Cortina but he knows about it. He is a tarantula. Did he tell you who bought it? That little man who bid against Stefan, he was only a lawyer.'

'No,' I said. 'He did not tell me. But he said the lawyer belonged to a Venetian firm that handled the financial affairs of big industrial concerns. I think he feared that a powerful hotel or tourist syndicate had bought it.'

'Perhaps,' she said. 'But it is strange. Big financiers do not pay fancy prices for places like Col da Varda.' She shrugged her shoulders. 'You ask yourself why I was prepared to pay so much, is that not so?'

'It certainly interests me,' I told her.

'But why?' she asked, and there was a note of irritation in her voice. 'Why are you so interested in my affairs? You are here to write a story for the cinema—so everyone is told. But you have my picture. You know my real name. You are interested enough in Col da Varda to attend the auction. What is all this to you? I insist that you tell me.'

I had my story ready now. That reference to my writing a script had given me the clue. The thing fell neatly into place. 'It's quite true about my writing a script for a film,' I said. 'And because I am a writer it is natural for me to be interested in anything unusual that I find happening around me. A writer bases everything he writes on people he has met, things that have happened to him, places that he's seen, stories that are told him. Everything an author writes, he has either experienced or seen or read about. I had your photograph. I did not know you or anything about you. You were just a signature to me, linked with the name Heinrich. And then I read that Heinrich Stelben was associated with a dancer named Carla Rometta. I meet you within a few hours of reading that. And then, next day, I find you prepared to pay a fantastic sum for Col da Varda, a property that was once owned by Heinrich Stelben. You must admit, I could hardly fail to be interested in such a strange sequence of events.'

She did not speak for a moment. She stood there, looking at me, her cigarette forgotten and a puzzled frown on her face. She seemed to accept the story, for all she eventually asked was, 'And the picture—how did you obtain that?'

I said, 'I have explained my interest. The only thing I haven't explained is how I came by the picture. Before I tell you that, perhaps you would be willing to satisfy my curiosity and tell me why you were prepared to pay as much as four million *lire* for Col da Varda? I am sorry,' I added. 'I have no right to ask— it is just that I am intrigued. It all seems so extraordinary.'

'I understand,' she said. 'You make a bargain—I tell you why I wanted Col da Varda and you tell me how the picture walked into your pocket. That is not gallant of you, for you are asking me to expose my heart. You have no right to ask me to do that. Whereas, I think I have a right to ask you about the picture— a picture I gave a long time ago to a very dear friend.' Her voice had dropped almost to a whisper.

I began to feel uncomfortable. After all it was none of my business. She had presumably been Heinrich Stelben's mistress. And she had a perfect right to go around buying up *slittovias* at absurd prices as often as she wished. And I intended lying to her anyway about how I had come by the photograph, just as I had lied to her already about my interest in the matter.

I was on the point of apologising and suggesting we continue down to Cortina, when she said, 'But I do not mind. So long as you tell no one. You promise?'

I nodded.

'The picture was taken just before the war. I was a dancer in Berlin. Heinrich was of the *Gestapo*. He was already married.

We had to be careful. But we were in love and we were happy. Then the war came and I stayed with him always. We were in many countries—Czechoslovakia, France, Austria, Hungary and then Italy. It was lovely.' Her voice was soft again now and her big dark eyes were looking past me into the sombre depths of the firs. 'Then Germany collapsed. Heinrich was arrested in a village on Lake Como. But he escaped and soon we were together again. He bought Col da Varda because—' Her eyes suddenly switched to my face searchingly. 'I wonder whether you will understand? You English are so cold. He bought it because that was where we had first met each other. It was January 1939—it was a warm sunny day and we sat out on the belvedere for hours, drinking and talking. For the rest of our holiday we met up there every day. And then, later that year, I followed him to Berlin, where he had arranged for me a contract to dance at one of the best night clubs in the city. For nearly three months we owned Col da Varda. It was heaven. Then those filthy *carabinieri* arrested him whilst I was in Venice. When he was sent to the Regina Coeli, I went to Rome to arrange his escape. But then he was handed over to the British. That was the end.' Her voice was no more than a breath, a sigh for something irrevocably lost.

She shrugged her shoulders and when she spoke again it was in her normal deep husky tones. 'That part of my life is finished. I shall not be faithful to Heinrich. I am not the faithful type. I have had too many men in my life. Even when he was alive, I was not faithful. But I loved him. That will sound strange to you—that I can sleep with several men and yet love only the one. But there it is. And that is why I wanted to buy Col da Varda. We had planned to convert the *rifugio* into a lovely little villa in the mountains. He had started on the alterations when he was arrested. Now that he is dead, I wanted it for my own. I have plenty of money. Heinrich did well in the *Gestapo*. He left me money in nearly every capital in Europe—real money— houses and jewellery—not bank accounts and worthless paper currency.' She looked up at me. 'There, now I have told you everything.'

I could not meet the reproachful gaze of her eyes. I felt embarrassed. She need not have told me everything in such detail. I sought refuge in a straightforward question: 'Why did you have Stefan Valdini bid for you at the auction?'

'Why, why, why!' She laughed at me. 'You are so full of questions. Why? Because I wished no publicity.'

'Of course,' I said. 'But why Valdini? He is—I don't know—he looks a crook.'

She laughed. 'But of course, my dear. How would he look otherwise? He is a crook. Poor Stefan! I am so sorry for him. And he is so faithful to me.' She was looking at me with a roguish smile now. 'You do not like Stefan, eh? He dresses too cheap—too loud. Oh, but you should have seen him before the war. He had a wardrobe of sixty suits and he had three hundred ties. Every suit, every tie more brilliant than the next. But now he has not so much. It was the Germans—they took many things from him. You will hear all about it. Now he has only twenty suits and eighty ties. He will tell you. He is not the man he was. He was quite a figure, you know, in the Eastern Mediterranean at one time.' She put her head quickly on one side and glanced up at me. 'Would it shock you to know something? Once I was one of his gairls.' Her imitation of the way Valdini said 'gairls' was perfect. 'There, now I *have* shocked you,' she said with a soft gurgle. 'But I have told you so much about myself, there is no reason why you should not know that. But he fell in love with me. Imagine—he was fool enough to fall in love with one of his own girls. Poor Stefan! He has never got over it. And now he is—how do you say?—on the down-slope. That makes me sorry for him.' She shrugged her shoulders and laughed quite gaily. 'There! I have answered all your interminable whys. Now you shall answer mine. How did you get my picture?'

'You will not believe it,' I said. 'It is too improbable. It was given me just before I left London,' I told her. 'We were in a bar, drinking. A friend of one of the party joined us. He had drunk a lot. When he heard I was returning to Italy, he gave me the photograph. He said he had got it from a German prisoner. He said it was of no interest to him now he was back. I was welcome to it. And if it intrigued me as much as it had intrigued him, he hoped I'd meet the girl. He never had. And that is all there is to it,' I finished lamely.

She looked at me searchingly. 'What was his name?' she asked.

'I don't know,' I replied. 'He was just a stray that joined our party.'

There was silence between us for a moment. The story seemed very thin. But perhaps its very thinness convinced her. 'Yes, it is possible. It was the British who questioned him after his arrest on Como. And why did you keep the picture with you? Did you like it so much?' She was laughing at me.

'Perhaps I thought I might meet the original,' I told her.

She smiled. 'And what do you think, now that you have met the original?' She laughed. 'But that is unfair. You have only just left your wife, is that not so? And you have met the Scarlet Woman. You are so English, my dear—so delightfully English. But we are friends—yes?' She took my arm happily. 'And you will be kind to my little Stefan, eh? Poor Stefan! He is such a frightful little man. But he cannot help himself. And when he likes people he is kind. I hope you will find him kind, Neil?' I don't know whether she was amused at her use of my christian name or at the possibility of my finding poor Stefan unkind. '*Avante!*' she said. 'We have talked so long, we must go fast to Cortina. I am having tea with a lovely Hungarian man.' And her expression as she said this was the equivalent of sticking out her tongue at me and my English ideas.

I had more confidence in my skis now and we made the run to Cortina at a quiet, steady pace. It was a fairly straightforward run. We crossed the road on the Cortina side of the Albergo Tre

Croci and dropped down a wooded valley till we joined the Faloria Olympic run. I left Carla at her hotel, the Majestico. 'We will meet again,' she said, as she let her hand rest in mine. 'But please do not tell any one about the things I have told you. I do not know why I told you so much—perhaps it was because you have a kind and understanding nature. And don't forget to be nice to my Stefan.' She laughed and withdrew her hand. '*Arrivederci.*' And she disappeared round the back of the hotel to remove her skis.

I went on to the *officio della poste*, thinking what a strange and disturbing woman she was. Heinrich must have been a gay devil to have maintained his hold on a woman like Carla even after his death.

After dispatching the cable to Engles, I ran into Keramikos. The Greek was just going into a shop to purchase wood carvings. I joined him and bought a pair of goat-herd book ends for Peggy and some little wooden animals for Michael. They were beautifully carved by local craftsmen. 'I like these shops,' Keramikos said. 'It makes me think of the old folk tales. In so many of the stories the little carved figures come to life during the night. I would like to be in the shop when that happens.'

'Are you going straight back?' I asked him as we left the shop.

'I think so,' he said. 'But it is not time yet. We have half an hour to wait for the bus. I suggest some tea.'

I readily agreed. It gave me an opportunity to find out what sort of a man he was and whether he had any particular reason for staying at Col da Varda. We went to a little café opposite the bus stop. It was hot in the cafe and very full of people relaxed after a strenuous day. A waitress brought us tea and I began to consider how best to lead the conversation round to himself. But before I had decided on my approach, he said, 'It is strange, that chalet. Have you considered what brings us there? Your friend, Wesson—he is simple. He is there for his film. But Valdini. Why does Valdini live up there? He is not an enthusiastic ski-er. He likes women and bright lights. He is a bird of the night. And there is Mayne. What is Mayne doing at Col da Varda? He is a sportsman. But he also likes women. You would not expect a man of his type to bury himself in a hut on a mountainside, except for exercise. But he does not go off on his skis at dawn and return at nightfall just to sleep. No, he goes to see an auction, as you did. It interests me so much why people do things.' He was staring at me unwinkingly from behind his thick-lensed glasses.

I nodded. 'Yes, it is interesting,' I agreed. And I added, 'And then there is yourself.'

'Ah, yes—then there is myself.' He nodded his round head and smiled as though amused at the thought of himself living at Col da Varda.

'Tell me, Mr Keramikos,' I said, 'why are you living there? Valdini says he thinks you prefer Cortina.'

He sighed. 'Perhaps I do. But then I also like solitude. There has been too much excitement in my life. It is quiet at Col da Varda. No, I am not going to talk about myself, Mr Blair. I prefer to gossip with you. Valdini? Valdini stays there for a purpose. He was to have bought the place for his friend, the Contessa. But I hear he was outbid this morning. Now, this is what interests me—will he continue to stay at the *rifugio* now that the place has been sold?'

'What's your guess?' I asked.

'My guess? I do not guess. I know. He will stay. Just as I know that you do not write a story for the films.'

His eyes were watching me closely. I felt annoyed. The conversation was being taken out of my hands. 'I have not written much yet,' I said, 'because I am absorbing the background.'

'Ah, yes—the background. Yes, that is a good explanation, Mr Blair. A writer can always explain anything he does, however strange, by saying that he seeks the background or the plot or the characters. But do you need an auction for your plot? Have you no better characters in your mind than the Contessa Forelli?

57

You see, I observe. And what I am observing is that you are more interested in what happens around you at Col da Varda than in your ski-ing story. Is that not so?'

'I am certainly interested,' I said defensively. Then with more attack: 'For instance, I am interested in you, Mr Keramikos.' He raised his eyebrows and smiled. 'You knew Mayne,' I said, 'before you met him last night.' It was a random thrust. I was not sure of myself.

He set down his teacup. 'Ah, you noticed that, eh? You are very observant, Mr Blair.' He considered for a moment. 'I wonder why you are so observant?' he mused. He drank thoughtfully as though considering the matter. 'Wesson is not observant. He is just a cameraman and he works hard taking pictures. Valdini, I know about. And Mayne, too. But you—I am not sure about you.' He seemed to hesitate. 'I will tell you something,' he said suddenly. 'And you will do well to think of it. You are quite right. I recognised Mayne. I had known him before. You do not know much about him, eh? How does he strike you?'

'He seems a pleasant enough fellow,' I replied. 'He is well read, friendly—has an attractive personality.'

He smiled. 'An engaging personality, eh? And he has travelled. He was in the United States during the prohibition days. Later he returned to England and in 1942 he joined the British Army.' He considered a moment. Then he said, 'Would it interest you to know, Mr Blair, that he deserted whilst serving in Italy?'

'How do you know?' I asked.

'He was useful to me in Greece,' Keramikos replied. 'For a time he operated a deserter gang in Naples, a bad crowd, composed of a variety of nationalities. They were cleaned up by the military police in the end. That was when he came to Athens. He operated on his own there as an UNRRA official. He was a very successful UNRRA official.' He smiled and took out a heavy silver watch. 'We must go,' he said, 'or you will miss your bus.' And he rose to his feet and paid the bill. I got up. The hum of voices, the clatter of crockery—all the sounds of the café—thrust themselves into my mind so that I wondered whether I had really understood what the Greek had told me.

Outside it was cold and the setting sun lit up the Dolomite peaks above the little town so that they flamed against the delicate blue of the sky. 'What was he doing for you in Greece?' I asked as we walked over to the bus stop.

But he held up his hand. 'I have said enough,' he answered. 'You are observant, Mr Blair. But do not be too observant. This is not England. The Austrian frontier is only a few miles away. Beyond lies Germany. Behind us is France. You were here in Italy before— but with your Army. You were part of a great organisation. But you are a civilian now and this is a strange, sick Europe. Things happen. Authority is a poor, bewildered official when things are out of control. Beyond all this luxury and all these men and women here who have grown fat on war, there is a vast human jungle. In that jungle, there is fear and starvation. It is the survival of the fittest. I tell you about Mayne because I would not like you to step outside this nice civilised Cortina and find yourself in that jungle.' He smiled at me as though he had passed some quite innocent remark. 'Tell Aldo for me, please, that I shall not be in to dinner.'

'But I thought you were coming back with me on the bus?' I said.

'No. I said that because I wished to talk to you alone. Remember your English saying—it takes all men to make a world. Remember also, please, that the world is not a good world just now. Good-night, Mr Blair.'

I watched his thick-set, powerful figure thrust its way through the crowded pavement till it was lost to view. Then I got on to the waiting bus with only my somewhat startled thoughts for company.

Joe Wesson was the only person in the *rifugio* when I returned. He looked at me sourly. 'I'd like to know what the hell you're playing at, Neil!' he grunted as he handed me a drink.

'Because I went to an auction this morning instead of getting on with the script?' I asked.

'Because, as far as I can see,' he replied, 'you haven't done a damn stroke of work since you arrived here. What's the matter? Won't your mind settle down to it?'

'I'll catch up after dinner,' I said. 'I've got the first part all worked out.'

'Good!' he said. 'I was beginning to get worried. Know what it's like. Seen other fellows in the same fix. It's not like camera work. It's got to be in your mind first.' For a man in such a hard business as films, he had an extraordinarily kind nature. 'How did the auction go?'

I told him.

'So that's why Valdini was so blasted miserable when I came in,' he said as I finished. 'Sicilian gangster, hm? Just what he looks like. You'd better keep clear of that damned Contessa of his, Neil. I went to Sicily once. All dust and flies—it was summer. Got involved with a little girl at the *pensione*. Her boy-friend came at me with a knife. But I was quicker then than I am now.'

We were the only two in to dinner. The big bar room seemed large and quiet—almost watchful. Our voices were never raised. We did not talk much during the meal. I was conscious of a nervous strain. I found myself wondering what the other three were doing—wondering what was happening in the world outside, wondering what was going to happen here. It was as though the hut, perched on the vast white shoulder of Monte Cristallo, was waiting for something.

I took myself off to my room immediately after dinner. I had to give Joe the impression I was doing some work. I wanted to work. I sat there at my typewriter, thinking how desperate Peggy and I had been before I had run into Engles in London that morning. I did not want that to happen again. This was my chance. All I had to do was produce a script that Engles would like.

But it just would not come. Every idea that came into my

mind was over-shadowed and crowded out by the thought of what was happening here in this hut. It was impossible to concentrate on fiction when the facts right under my nose were so absorbing. For the hundredth time I tried to figure out why Engles was interested in the place. Valdini and the Contessa were now clear in my mind. But Mayne and Keramikos? Was it true what Keramikos had told me about Mayne? And why had he told me? Why had he warned me? And who had bought Col da Varda, and why?

I stared blankly at the keys of my typewriter, smoking cigarette after cigarette in a frenzy of frustration. Why didn't I ignore the whole thing and get on with the script? I cursed my honesty and damned Engles for employing me as watch-dog to a group of highly questionable characters and not as a straightforward script writer.

It was cold in the room, even with the electric heater on. The moon had risen and, beyond the reflected gleam of the unshaded electric light bulb, I could see the frosted white of the world outside my window. It came right up to the window, that cold, unfriendly world. The snow was thick on the window-sill—thick and glistening white. And from the roof a great curve of snow hung suspended like icing on a cake, ending in a long, pointed icicle.

At length I gave it up. It was no good thinking about writing a script when so many queries crowded my brain. I began to hammer out on the typewriter yet another report for Engles, this time on Keramikos. Whilst I was recalling that tea-time conversation, I heard the *slittovia*. It came up and went down again three separate times within an hour. I heard voices downstairs in the bar. Then, about ten, there was the tramp of heavy boots on the stair boards, voices said good-night, doors banged. Joe poked his head round the door of my room. 'How's it going?' he enquired.

'All right, thanks,' I told him.

'Good. It's all clear downstairs now. They've all gone to bed. It's warmer down there, if you're working late.'

I thanked him. He went into his room. I heard him moving about for several minutes. Then all was quiet. The hut had settled down to sleep. The sound of Joe's snores began to come through the match-boarding as clear as though he were asleep in the room.

I put the lid on my typewriter and got up. I was stiff with cold. I hurried into the warmth of my bed. But I could not sleep. Thoughts kept chasing through my mind.

Whether I dozed off or not I do not know. All I know is that I was suddenly awake. And it was much later. The moon had moved round and was shining across the room on to the white enamel-ware of the wash-stand. The rhythmic snore of Joe's breathing was just the same. The hut was quiet. Yet something was different. I lay huddled in the warmth of the bedclothes looking about me, conscious of that strange watchfulness I had felt in old houses when as a child I had lain awake in the dark.

I tried to go to sleep again. But I could not. I thought of the bar downstairs. I could do with a cognac or two. I got up and put two sweaters and my ski suit on over my pyjamas. I had just finished dressing when I noticed something different about the window. I went over to it and peered out. The great overhanging mass of snow with the icicle on the end was gone. The sound of it falling must have been the cause of my waking.

I was turning away when I saw a figure moving across the belvedere. The moon gave his body a long shadow that lay full across the boards of the platform. I peered down as it hurried silently down the steps and was lost to view behind the wooden balustrade. When it was gone I blinked my eyes and wondered if it had ever really been there. It had been a tall figure.

I hesitated. It was nothing to do with me. A boy-friend of Anna's perhaps. Her bright, laughing eyes might well do more than flirt with visitors as she brought them food and drinks. I looked at my watch. It was after two.

I suppose it was the fact that I was actually dressed and wide awake that determined me. I was suddenly outside my room and slipping quietly down the stairs in stockinged feet.

The large bar room was a ghostly space of silence in the wide shafts of moonlight. I crossed it quickly and opened the door. Outside it was cold and bright with the moon. I put my shoes on and tiptoed across the belvedere and down the steps on to the snow path that led up from the *slittovia*.

I was in shadow here, for the platform of the belvedere was higher than my head and the path ran close beside it. I stopped to consider. There was no sign of the figure I had seen from my window. The *rifugio*, viewed from this angle, had a perfectly straight façade. The great pine piles on which it was built were so tall that it was possible for a man to walk underneath by bending slightly. Halfway along, the pine supports ceased and the base of the hut became concrete. This was the concrete housing of the *slittovia* plant. It had a broad window looking straight down the sleigh track. I could see the dark square of it despite the fact that it was in shadow. Just below the window was a slit and the cable that emerged from it was just visible. Opposite the window, a wooden platform had been built out on to the actual slope of the trackway to enable passengers to alight from the sleigh.

I was cold, standing there, and I began to regard myself as more than a little foolish, wandering about in the snow after shadows at two in the morning. But just as I was considering returning to the bar for a drink, I saw a slight movement where the pine supports gave place to the concrete machine housing. I watched closely. For a while there was no further movement, but now I could make out a darker shadow against the concrete. It was the shadow of a man standing very still almost underneath the flooring of the bar.

I froze to complete stillness. I was in shadow. As long as I did not move he might not see me. I must have stayed like that for perhaps a minute, debating whether I dare risk moving right under the platform, for, if he came back towards me, he was bound to see me. Before I could make up my mind, however, the shadow began to move. It came out from underneath the *rifugio* and moved along the concrete face of the machine-room. He was quite clear to me now in silhouette against the white snow of the firs beyond. He was a shortish, thick-set man. He was not a bit like the man I had seen cross the belvedere. He stopped by the window of the machine-room and peered in.

I climbed quickly over the crisp-piled snow and got in under the platform. Then I made my way carefully along under the hut until I was close to the concrete section. I peered out. The man was still there, his body a dark shadow by the window.

A light suddenly shone out from the machine-room. It was the moving light of a torch and it rested for a moment on the face of the watcher. I recognised it instantly. It was Keramikos. I stepped back behind one of the supporting piles. I was only just in time. The Greek slipped back into cover. But he was not quick enough. The sound of footsteps crunched in the frosty snow and the torchlight was shone straight on to him. 'I have been expecting you.' I could not see the speaker. He was just a voice and the glare of the white circle of his torch. He spoke in German, the lighter German of Austria.

Keramikos stepped forward. 'If you were expecting me,' he replied in German, 'there's no point in my continuing this game of hide-and-seek.'

'None whatever,' was the reply. 'Come inside. You may as well look at the place whilst you're here and there are some things we might talk over.'

The beam of the torch swung away and the two figures moved beyond my line of vision. A door was closed and their voices immediately ceased.

I slipped out of my hiding-place and moved quietly to where Keramikos had been standing. I knelt down to peer in through the window, so that my head would not appear at the level expected if the torch were shone on the window again.

It was a weird scene. The torch was held so that the light of it fell full on Keramikos. His face was white in the glare of it and his shadow sprawled grotesquely on the wall behind him. They sat opposite each other on the great cable drum. The stranger was smoking, but he had his back to me, so that the slight glow as he drew on his cigarette did not show me his face. Except for the one wall, the room was in half darkness, and the machinery showed only as shadowy bulks huddled in their concrete bedding.

I remained watching till my knees began to ache. But they just sat there talking. They did not move. There were no excited gestures. They seemed quite friendly. The window had small panes set in steel frames. I could not hear a word.

I crawled across the platform and stepped over the cable. The snow crunched noisily under my feet. I was at the very top of the sleigh track. It dropped almost from under my feet, a snowy slash between the dark firs. I crossed it and went round the corner of the concrete housing to the door, which was under the wooden flooring of the *rifugio*. It was closed. Very carefully I lifted the latch and pulled it towards me.

Through a half inch slit I could see that the scene had not changed. They were still seated, facing each other, with Keramikos blinking like an owl in the glare of the torch. '. . . loosen off this cog,' the stranger was saying, still in Austrian. He shone the torch on a heavy, grease-coated cog that engaged the main driving cog on the rim of the cable drum. 'Then all we have to do is to knock it out when the sleigh has started down. It will be on the steepest part. There will be an accident. Then I will close the *rifugio*. Afterwards we can search without fear of interruption.'

'You are certain it is here?' Keramikos asked.

'Why else did Stelben buy the place? Why else did his mistress want to buy it? It's here all right.'

Keramikos nodded. Then he said, 'You didn't trust me before. Why should you trust me now? And why should I trust you?'

'Case of necessity,' was the reply.

65

Keramikos seemed to consider. 'It is neat,' he said. 'That would dispose of Valdini and the Contessa. And then—' He stopped abruptly. He was gazing straight at me. 'I thought you shut the door. There's a draught coming through it.' He got to his feet. The torch followed him as he moved towards the door.

I slipped quickly into the shadows among the piles. The door was thrust open and the light from the torch made the snow glisten. I peered out from behind the support that sheltered me. Keramikos was examining the ground outside the door. He bent down and felt the snow.

'Anything wrong?' The other's voice sounded hollow from the interior of the concrete room.

'No,' replied Keramikos. 'I suppose it was not latched properly.' He closed the door. It was dark again and the silence of the night drew closer to me.

A few minutes later they came out. A key grated in the lock of the door and the two shadowy figures disappeared along the path that led back to the belvedere.

4

My Shroud is Driven Snow

I waited there for perhaps half an hour. It was very cold and rather eerie in that white silence with only the stars for company. But I was determined to take no chances. Keramikos must not see me return. And I had plenty to occupy my mind as I stood there in the chill darkness.

But at last the cold drove me in. I moved quietly, keeping to the shadows. I crossed the belvedere in the shadow of a fir tree that had crept across it, for the moon was getting low. The bar room seemed warm and friendly after the cold of the night. I crossed to the bar and poured myself a stiff, neat cognac. It was fire in my chilled stomach. I poured myself another.

'I have been waiting for you, Mr Blair.'

I nearly dropped the glass. The voice came from the shadows in the corner by the piano. I swung round.

It was Keramikos. He was seated on the piano stool. His figure was shadowy in the darkness of the corner, but his glasses reflected the single bar light. He looked like a great toad.

'Why?' I asked, and my voice trembled.

'Because I saw the print of a pair of shoes outside that door. When I touched the prints the snow was wet. It had to be either you or Valdini. Valdini's room is next to mine. He snores. Your door was open. That was careless, I think.' He got up. 'Would you be so kind as to pour me a cognac. It has been cold, waiting for you. Though not as cold, doubtless, as you found it, waiting outside.'

I poured him a drink.

He came over and took it from my hand. His hand was large and hairy. It was much steadier than mine.

'Your health,' he said with a smile and raised the glass.

I did not feel in the mood for such a gesture.

'Why did you wait up for me?' I asked. 'And where's the Austrian fellow?'

'The Austrian fellow?' He peered at me through his glasses. 'You did not see him, eh?' He nodded as though satisfied about something. 'He's gone,' he said. 'He does not know you were there. I waited up for you because there are some questions I would like to ask you.'

'And there are a few I'd like to ask you,' I said.

'I've no doubt,' he replied curtly. 'But you would be a fool to expect me to answer them.' He considered me for a moment as he poured himself another drink. 'You speak German, eh?' he asked.

'Yes,' I said.

'You were listening to our conversation. It is not good, Mr Blair, to meddle in matters that are of no concern to you.' His voice was quiet, his tone reasonable. It was difficult to realise that there was an implied threat.

'Murder is a matter that concerns everybody,' I responded sharply.

'The *slittovia*, eh? So you heard that. What else did you hear?' There was no mistaking the menace in his voice now, though the tone was still quiet.

'God!' I cried. 'Isn't that enough?'

He gazed at the drink in his glass. 'You should not leap to conclusions, Mr Blair,' he said. 'You only heard part of the conversation.'

'Listen, Keramikos,' I said. 'You can't fool me by suggesting that I didn't hear all the conversation. That little scrap was complete in itself. The Austrian was proposing cold-blooded murder.'

'And do you know why?'

'Because you're searching for something,' I snapped back, angered by the casualness of his manner. 'What is there to search for that's so important you'll commit murder in order not to be interrupted?'

'That, my friend, is none of your business,' he replied quietly. 'If you believe you have correctly interpreted the scrap of conversation you have overheard, then I suggest you avoid travelling on the *slittovia*. And confine your curiosity to your own affairs. My advice to you is—get on with your film story.'

'How the hell do you expect me to write a film script in these circumstances,' I cried.

He laughed. 'That is for you to consider. In the meantime, be a little less curious. Good-night, Mr Blair.' He nodded to me curtly and walked out of the room. I heard his feet on the stairs and then the sound of a door closing.

I finished my drink and went up to my room. The door stood open as Keramikos had said. I was certain I had closed it when I left. The room looked just the same. There was no indication that any one had been in it. I sat down on the bed and switched on the electric heater. I was puzzled and, I think, a little frightened. Keramikos had not been angry, but there had been a quiet menace in his words that was even more disturbing.

To try and sleep was out of the question. I decided to add to my report to Engles. I picked up my typewriter and lifted the cover. I was just going to remove the sheet of paper on which I had already typed the day's report when I noticed that the top of it had been caught between the cover and the base. The paper was torn and dirtied by the catches. Now I am always most careful to adjust the paper so that this does not happen when I am putting my typewriter away with copy in it. It is quite automatic. Somebody had read that report and had failed to adjust the paper properly before putting the lid back on to the typewriter. I made a quick search of the room. My things were all in place, but here and there they had been moved slightly—a bottle of ink at the bottom of my suitcase was on its side, some letters in a writing case were in a different order and several other small things were out of place. I became certain that Keramikos had searched my room. But why had he left the door open? Was he trying to frighten me?

The only thing that mattered was the report to Engles. Fortunately there was no address on it. It read like part of a diary. It was quite innocuous, merely recording my conversations with Carla and Keramikos that afternoon. But it showed my interest. I suddenly remembered that cable from Engles. But it was all right. It was in the wallet in my pocket. The photograph of Carla was also there.

I sat down then and penned an account of the night's happenings for Engles.

When I came down to breakfast, after only a short sleep, I found Mayne at the piano. 'Know this, Blair?' he asked. He was as full of sunlight as the morning. The notes rippled from his fingers like the sound of a mountain stream.

'Handel's *Water Music*,' I said.

He nodded. He had a beautiful touch. 'Do you like Rossini for breakfast?' he asked. And without waiting for an answer, he slid into the overture of *The Barber of Seville*. Gay, subtle humour, full of mockery and laughter, filled the sunny room. 'There is more of Italy in this music, I think, than in the works of all her other composers put together,' he said. 'It is gay, like Anna here.' The girl had just come in to lay the breakfast and she flashed him a smile at the sound of her name. 'Do you know this piece, Anna?' he asked in Italian, switching into the first act. She listened for a second, her head held prettily on one side. Then she nodded. 'Sing it then,' he said.

She smiled and shook her head in embarrassment.

'Go on. I'll start again. Ready?' And she began to sing in a sweet soprano. It was gay and full of fun.

'That is the Italian side of her,' he said to me through the music. He suddenly left her flat and thumped into the priest scene. 'But she does not understand this,' he shouted to me. 'She is Austrian now—and a good Catholic. This mocks at the Church. Only the Italians would mock at their Church. Here it is—the foolish, knavish priest enters.' The notes crashed out mockingly.

He struck a final chord and swung round on the stool. 'What are you doing today, Blair?' he asked. 'Yesterday you introduced me to a very good entertainment at that auction. Today I would like to return your kindness. I would like to take you ski-ing. It is early in the season and there is a lot of snow still to fall. We should not waste a fine day like this. Besides, the forecast is for snow later. What about coming up Monte Cristallo with me?'

'I'd like to,' I said. 'But I feel I ought to do some work.'

'Nonsense,' he said. 'You can work all this evening. Besides, you ought to have a look at one of the real mountains up here. I can show you a glacier and some very fine avalanche slopes. Your fat friend is only taking pictures of the ordinary ski runs. You ought to take a look at the real mountains. There's good film stuff up there.'

'Really,' I said, 'I must work.'

He shrugged his shoulders. 'My God, you take life seriously. What does a day more or less matter? You should have been born in Ireland. Life would have been more fun for you.' He swung back to the piano and began thumping out one of Elgar's more solid pieces, looking at me over his shoulder with a twinkle in his eyes. He quickly changed into a gay Irish air. 'If you change your mind,' he said, 'I'll be leaving about ten.'

The others were drifting in now, attracted by the music and the smell of bacon and eggs frying. Conscious of a growing audience, Mayne switched to Verdi and began to play seriously again. Only Joe was not interested. He looked tired and liverish. 'Does he have to make a damned row so early in the morning?' he grumbled in my ear. 'Like talking at breakfast—can't stand it.' His face looked grey in the hard sunlight and the pouches under his eyes were very marked.

The mail came up, after breakfast, on the first sleigh. With it was a cable from Engles. It read: *Why Mayne Keramikos unmentioned previously. Full information urgent. Engles.*

A few minutes later Mayne came over to me. He had his ski boots on and was carrying a small haversack. 'What about changing your mind, Blair?' he said. 'We needn't make it a long day. Suppose we're back by three, would that be all right for you? It's not much fun going for a ski run by one's self.'

I hesitated. I did want to get some writing done. On the other hand, I couldn't bear the thought of being cooped up in the hut all day. And Engles wanted information about Mayne. It would be a good opportunity to find out about the man. 'All right,' I said. 'I'll be ready in about ten minutes.'

'Good!' he said. 'I'll have Aldo get your skis ready. No need to worry about food. We'll get it at the hotel at Carbonin.' His eagerness was infectious. Any one less like a man who had once led a gang of deserters I could not imagine. And suddenly I did not believe a word Keramikos had said. It was too fantastic. The Greek had just been trying to divert my attentions from himself.

As I came down in my ski suit and boots, Joe raised his eyebrows. He did not say anything, but bent over the camera he was loading. 'Care to lend me that small camera of yours, Joe?' I asked.

He looked up. 'No,' he said. 'I wouldn't trust that camera to any one. Why? Think you can get some shots that I can't? Where are you off to?'

'Monte Cristallo,' I told him. 'Mayne says he can show me a glacier and some fine avalanche slopes. I thought they might produce some good shots. It would be grander stuff than you can get down here.'

Joe laughed. 'Shows how little you know about camera work,' he said. 'It's all a matter of angles and light. I haven't been more than a thousand yards from this hut, but I've got everything. I don't need to go trapesing all over the Dolomites to get my background.'

'I wish I had your sublime self-confidence,' I said.

I suppose I had spoken with a shade of bitterness, for he looked up and patted my arm. 'It'll come,' he said. 'It'll come. A couple of successes and you'll never listen to advice again—until it's too late. I'm at the top now. Nobody can teach me anything about cameras. But it won't last. In a few years' time younger men will come along with new ideas which I shan't be able to see, and that'll be that. It's the way it goes in this racket. Engles will tell you the same.'

I left him then and went out on to the belvedere. Mayne was waiting for me there. Just a couple of successes! It was so easy to talk about it. And I hadn't even begun a script. The wood of my skis was actually warm to the touch as they stood propped against the balustrade in the sun. But though the sun was warm, it made little or no impression on the snow, which remained hard and frozen.

We started up across virgin snow until we hit the track to the Passo del Cristallo. It was not really a track—just a few ski marks lightly dusted over with a powder of snow that had drifted across them during the night. The run looked as though it was little used. 'You know the way, I suppose?' I asked Mayne.

He stopped and turned his head. 'Yes. I haven't done it this year. But I've done it often before. You don't need to worry about having no guide. It's quite straightforward until we get up near the top of the pass. There's a nasty bit of climbing to do to get to the top of it. We'll be just on ten thousand feet up there. We may have to do the last bit without skis. Then there's the glacier. That's about a kilometre. There should be plenty of snow on it. After that it's quite a simple run down to Carbonin.' He turned and plodded on ahead of me again, thrusting steadily with his sticks.

I think if I had had the sense to look at the map before we started out, I should never have gone on that particular run. It is not a beginner's run. And it looks a bit frightening even on the map. There's at least a kilometre on the way up to the glacier

73

marked with interrupted lines, denoting 'difficult itinerary.' Then there is the glacier itself. And both on the way up from Col da Varda and on the way down to Carbonin, the red hachures of avalanche slopes are shown falling down towards the track on every side.

As we climbed steadily upwards, zig-zagging in places because of the steepness of the entrance to the pass, I had a glimpse of what was to come. The outer bastions of Monte Cristallo towered above us to the left, a solid wall of jagged edges. To our right, a great field of snow swept precipitously down towards us, like a colossal sheet pinned to the blue sky by a single jagged peak. It was across the lower slopes of this that we were steadily climbing. There was no track at all now. The wind whistling up the pass had completely obliterated the marks of the previous day's ski-ers. We were alone in a white world and ahead of us the pass rose in rolling downs of snow to the sharp rock teeth that marked the top of the pass. The sunlight had a brittle quality and the bare rock outcrops above us had no warmth in their colouring. They looked cold and black.

I could, I suppose, have turned back then. But Mayne had a confident air. He was never at a loss for direction. And I was feeling quite at ease now on my skis. The stiffness had worn off and, though the going was hard and I was out of training, I felt quite capable of making it. It was only the solitude and the lurking belief that we should have had a guide on a run of this sort that worried me.

Once I did say, 'Do you think we ought to go over the top on to the glacier without a guide?'

Mayne was making a standing turn at the time. He looked down at me, clearly amused. 'It's not half as bad as landing on a shell-torn beach,' he grinned. Then more seriously, 'We'll turn back if you like. But we're nearly up to the worst bit. See how you make out on that. I'd like to get to the top at any rate and look down to the glacier. But I don't want to do it alone.'

'Of course not,' I said. 'I'm quite all right. But I just feel we ought to have had a guide.'

'Don't worry,' he said quite gaily. 'It's almost impossible to lose your way on this run. Except for a spell at the top, you're in the pass the whole time.'

Soon after this it began to get very steep. The pass towered ahead of us, itself like the face of an avalanche slope. And on each side of us, we were hemmed in by real avalanche slopes that swept high above the pass to the dark crests. It was no longer possible to zig-zag up the slope. It was too steep. We began side-stepping. The snow was hard like ice and at each step it was necessary to stamp the ski edge into the frozen snow to get a grip. Even so, it was only just the inside edge of the ski that bit into the snow. It was hard, tiring work. But there was nothing dangerous about it so long as the skis were kept firm and exactly parallel to the contour of the slope.

For what seemed ages, I saw nothing of the scenery. Indeed, I did not even look up to see where we were going. I just blindly followed the marks of Mayne's ski edges. My eyes were fixed entirely on my rhythmically stamping feet, my mind concentrated on maintaining my skis at the correct angle. The higher we climbed the more dangerous it became if the skis faced fractionally down the slope and began to slide. So we progressed in complete silence, save for the stamp of our skis and the crunch as they bit into the icy snow.

'Snow's drifted up here,' came Mayne's voice from above. 'Have to take our skis off soon.'

A few feet higher up I saw the first sign of rock. It was a small outcrop, smooth and ice-rounded. Then I was up with Mayne. The slope was less now. I stood up and looked about me, blinking my eyes in the sunlight. We were standing on the rim of a great white basin. The snow simply fell away from under our feet. The slope up which we had climbed fanned out and mingled with the avalanche slopes that came in from either side. I could scarcely believe that those were our ski marks climbing up out of the basin—the tracks showed clearly like a little railway line mapped out on white paper.

I looked ahead of us. There was nothing but smoothed rock and jagged tooth-like peaks. 'That's Popena,' Mayne said, pointing to a single peak rising sharply almost straight ahead of us. 'The track runs just under that to the left.' The sun was cold—the air strangely visible, like a white vapour. It was a cold, rarified air and I could feel my heart pumping against my ribs.

A little farther on, we removed our skis. It was just drift snow here and, with our skis over our shoulders, we made steady progress, choosing the rock outcrops and avoiding the drifts.

At last we stood at the top of the pass.

The main peaks were still above us. But they only topped our present position by a few hundred feet. We were looking out upon a world of jumbled rocks—black teeth in white gums of snow. It was cold and silent. Nothing lived here. Nothing had ever lived here. We might have been at one of the Poles or in some forgotten land of the Ice Age. This was the territory of Olympian Gods. The dark peaks jostled one another, battling to be the first to pierce the heavens, and all about them their snow skirts dropped away to the world below, that nice comfortable world where human beings lived. 'Wesson should bring his camera up here,' I said, half to myself.

Mayne laughed. 'It'd kill him. He'd have heart failure before he got anywhere near the top.'

It was cold as soon as we stood still. The wind was quite strong and cut through our windbreakers. It drove the snow across the rocks on which we stood like dust. It was frozen, powdery snow. I could sift it through my gloved hands like flour. Here and there along the ridges a great curtain of it would be lifted up by the wind and would drift across the face of the rock like driven spume. There was no sign of the blue sky that had looked so bright and gay from Col da Varda. The air was white with light.

Mayne pointed to the great bulk of Monte Cristallo. The sky had darkened there and the top of the mountain was gradually being obscured as though by a veil. The sun was only visible as an iridescent light. 'Going to snow soon,' he said. 'Better be moving. I'd like to get across the glacier before it comes on thick. Later it doesn't matter. We'll be in the pass. If it looks bad after lunch, we'd better come back by Lake Misurina.'

He was so confident and I was so reluctant to face the steep descent into that basin that I raised no objection to going forward. Soon we reached the glacier and put on our skis. It was very little different to the rock slopes that encompassed it, for it was covered with a blanket of snow. Only here and there was there any sign of the ice that formed the foundation for the snow. The going was much easier now. The slope was quite gentle and our skis slid easily across the snow with only an occasional thrust of our sticks. The brightness slowly dimmed and the sky became heavy and leaden. I did not like the look of it. You feel so small and unimportant up there in the mountains. And it's not a pleasant feeling. You feel that one rumble of thunder and the elements can sweep you out of existence. One by one the peaks that surrounded the glacier in a serrated edge were blotted out.

We were barely halfway across the glacier when it began to snow. At first it was just a few flakes drifting across our path in the wind. But it grew rapidly thicker. It came in gusts, so that one moment it was barely possible to see the edges of the glacier and the next it was almost clear, so that it was possible to see the encircling crests that swept upwards to bury their peaks in the grey sky.

Mayne had increased the pace. I became very conscious of the pounding of my heart. Whether it was the continued exercise at that altitude or nervousness I do not know. Probably both. In all that world of grey and white, the only friendly thing was Mayne's back and the slender track of his skis that seemed to link us like a rope across the snow.

At last we were across the glacier. The snow was falling steadily now, a slanting, driven fall that stung the face and clung to the eyes. The slope became steeper. We began to travel fast, zig-zagging down through tumbled slopes of soft, fresh snow. It became steeper still and the pace even faster.

I kept in the actual track of Mayne's skis. Sometimes I lost sight of him in the snow. But always there were the ski tracks to follow. The only sounds were the steady hiss of driven snow and the friendly biting sound of my skis. I followed blindly. I had no idea where we were going. But we were going downhill and that was all I cared. How Mayne managed to keep a sense of direction in that murk I do not know.

I suddenly found him standing still, waiting for me. His face was hardly recognisable, it was so covered in snow. He looked like a snow man. 'It's coming on thick,' he said as I came up with him. 'Have to increase the pace. Is that all right with you?'

'That's all right,' I said. Anything so long as we got down as quickly as possible. The smoke of our breath was whipped away by the wind.

'Stick to my tracks,' he said. 'Don't diverge or we'll lose touch with each other.'

'I won't,' I assured him.

'It's good, fast going now,' he added. 'We'll be out of the worst of it soon.' He stepped back into his tracks where they finished abruptly and pushed off ahead of me again.

I was a bit worried as we started off, for I did not know how much better Mayne was as a ski-er than myself. And ski-ing across fresh snow is not the same as ski-ing down one of the regular runs. The ski runs are flattened so that you can put a brake on your speed by snow-ploughing—pressing the skis out with the heels so that they are thrusting sideways with the points together, like a snow-plough. You can stem, too. But in fresh snow, you can't do that. You adjust your speed by varying the steepness of the run. If a slope is too steep for you, you take it

78

in a series of diagonals. You can only go fast and straight on clean snow if you can do a real Christi—and the Christiana turn is the most difficult of all, a jump to clear the skis from their tracks and a right angle turn in mid-air.

I mention this because it worried me at the time. I have never got as far in ski-ing as the Christiana turn and, if Mayne could Christi, I wondered if he would realise that I could not. I wished I had mentioned the fact to him when he suggested increasing the pace.

But soon my only concern was to keep my skis in his tracks. We were going in an oblique run down the shoulder of a long hill. Mayne was taking a steep diagonal and we were running at something over thirty miles an hour through thick, driving snow. It is not an experience I wish to repeat. I could have followed the line of his skis on a gentler run and zig-zagged down to meet it when I got too far above his line. But that would slow my pace and I did not dare fall too far behind. As it was, the snow was quite thick in his tracks by the time I followed on. In places they were being half obliterated in a matter of seconds.

The snow whipped at my face and blinded my eyes. I was chilled right through with the cold and the speed. In places the snow was very soft and Mayne's skis had bitten deep into it. This made it difficult for me at times to retain my balance.

At the end of that long diagonal run, I found him waiting for me, a solitary figure in that blur of white and grey, the track of his skis running right up to him like a little railway. I stepped out of his tracks just before I reached him and stopped by running uphill. I looked at him and saw that he had brought himself up standing by a Christi. A wide arc of ploughed-up snow showed where he had made the turn.

'Just wanted to find out whether you were all right on a Christi,' he called to me.

I shook my head. 'Sorry!' I shouted back.

'All right. Just wanted to know. We'll soon be in the pass now. That'll give us some shelter. I'll go easy and stick to diagonals.'

He turned and started off again. I joined his ski tracks and followed on. We reached a steeper part, made two diagonals down it, with standing turns at the end of each. Then followed a long clear run across a sloping field of snow.

It was like a plateau—like a white sloping desk-top. As I came to the edge of it, I realised suddenly that it was going to drop away sharply. I remember noticing how the edges of Mayne's ski tracks stood out against the grey void of falling snow beyond the lip. Then I was over the edge, plunging, head well down, along tracks that ran straight as a die down a long, very steep hillside of snow.

I should have fallen before my speed became too great. But I had confidence in Mayne's judgment. I felt sure that the steep descent must end in a rise. Mayne would never have taken it straight otherwise. The wind pressed in an icy blanket against my face. Already I was travelling at a tremendous pace. The snow was thick and I could not see more than forty or fifty yards ahead. I kept my legs braced and supple at the knees and let myself go. It was exhilarating, like going downhill on the Giant Racer.

Then suddenly the snow lifted a little. Mayne's tracks ran down into the bottom of a steep-sided little valley of snow. The opposite slope of that valley seemed to rise almost sheer. It was like a wall of snow, and I was hurtling towards it. And at the bottom I could see the flurry of churned-up snow where Mayne had been forced to do a Christi. His tracks ran on away to the right along the floor of the valley.

My heart leaped in my throat. There was nothing I could do about it but hope that my skis would make the opposite side and not dig their points in. I dared not fall now. I was going too fast.

The snow slope of the opposite side of the valley rose to meet me with incredible speed. It seemed to pounce at me. I braced my legs for the upward thrust of my skis. My ski points lifted as I hit the floor of the valley. Then the snow slope beyond flung itself at me. A cold, wet world closed about me in an icy smother.

I was suddenly still. All the wind was knocked out of my body. I could not breathe. My mouth and nostrils were blocked with cold snow. My legs felt twisted and broken. I could not move them. I sobbed for the air I needed.

I fought to clear my face. I got my hand to my mouth and scraped away the snow. Still I could not breathe. I panicked and lashed out with my arms. Everywhere I felt soft snow that yielded and then packed hard as I fought against it.

I realised then that I was buried. I was frightened. I fought upwards with my hands, gripped in a frenzy of terror. Then the grey light of the sky showed through a hole in the snow and I breathed in air in great sobbing gulps.

As soon as I had recovered my wind, I tried to loosen my legs from the snow in which they were buried. But the ski points had dug themselves firmly in and I could not move them. I tried to reach down to loosen the skis off my boots. But I could not reach that far, for every time I tried to raise myself in order to bend down, my arm sank to the shoulder in the snow. It was very soft.

I tried to find my sticks. I needed the webbed circle of them to support me. But I could not find them. I had removed my hands from the thongs when I was fighting for air and they were buried deep under me. I scraped a clear patch in the snow around me and slewed my body round, bending down whilst still lying in the snow. It took all my energy and gave my twisted legs much pain. But at last I was able to reach the spring clip of my left ski. I pressed it forward and felt immediate release from the pain in my leg as my boot freed itself from the ski. I moved my leg about in the snow. It seemed all right. Then I did the same with the other foot. That too seemed sound.

I lay back exhausted after that. The snow fell steadily on me from above. The wind kept drifting it into the hole in which I was lying, so that I had to be continually pressing the fresh snow back in order not to be smothered.

When I had recovered from the effort of freeing my legs, I began to set about trying to get on to my feet. But it was quite impossible. The instant I put pressure on the snow with either my hands or my legs, I simply sank into it. It was like a bog. I was only safe as long as I continued to lie at full length. Once I struggled into a sitting position and managed to grasp the end of one of my skis. With this I levered myself on to both feet at the same time.

Immediately I sank in the snow up to my thighs. I was utterly exhausted by the time I had extricated myself. There is nothing in the world more exhausting than trying to get up in soft snow and I was tired from the long run in the first place.

I lay on my back, panting. My muscles felt like soft wire. They had no resilience in them. I decided to wait for Mayne. He would follow his ski tracks back. Or would they be obliterated? Anyway, he would remember the way he had come. It might be a little time yet. But he would soon realise that I was not behind him. He might have to climb a bit. How long had I been there? It seemed hours.

I lay back and closed my eyes and tried to pretend that this wasn't wet snow, but a comfortable bed. The sweat dried on me, making my skin feel cold. The snow was melting under me with the heat of my body and the wet was coming through my ski suit. Fresh snow drifted across my face.

I thought of that long steep descent that had ended so ignominiously here in the snow. And then I remembered with a terrible feeling of panic how Mayne's ski tracks had turned sharply along the floor of the valley. That flurry of ploughed-up snow! Mayne had done a Christi there. Yet only a few minutes earlier he had stopped expressly to find out whether or not I could do a Christi.

The truth dawned on me slowly as I lay there in the snow. *Mayne had meant this to happen.*

And I knew then that he would not come back.

5

Back Across the Glacier

When I realised that Mayne would not come back, I had a moment of complete panic. Half-a-dozen times I tried to get on to my feet. But arms and legs were simply swallowed by the soft snow. At the last attempt, I suddenly felt utter exhaustion sweep over me. I put my hand out to hold myself in a sitting position so that my head would remain above the edge of the hole in which I lay. I was afraid of that hole. It was like a grave. The fresh snow drifted so persistently over the crisp edges of it. I felt smothered there. But my hand sank into that feather-bed of snow and I toppled slowly over on to my side.

I lay still for a moment after that. My muscles relaxed. A great feeling of lethargy stole over me. Why should I care? Why should I struggle? I could just lie there and go to sleep. I wasn't cold any more—not for the moment. The snow had got inside my clothes and melted, but my blood had warmed my wet under-clothes. Only my hand was cold where it was buried under me.

I began to move it about in order to extricate it. And then my fingers touched something hard—hard and rounded. With sudden renewed energy I searched about with my frozen fingers. It was the top of one of my sticks. Hope, and that sudden relief that hope brings, flooded through me. I lay with my head buried in the snow-caked sleeve of my left arm and sobbed with relief. One of my sticks! Anything seemed possible if only I could get hold of my sticks again.

And with hope came reason. I lay there for a moment planning my moves carefully. I must husband my strength. To get this one stick out. That was the first thing. Then search for the other with my skis.

I rolled over on to my stomach and began to dig with my hands. I dug all round the stick. And at last I freed it. I pulled it clear and wiped the snow from it. It was like the sight of a ship to a drowning man. I had no feeling in my right hand. I took my wet glove off and breathed on my hand and rubbed it. The circulation began to tingle and burn in the finger-ends.

I pressed the end of the stick into the snow. It was wonderful to feel the webbed circle of it pack the snow down and hold my weight. I thrust myself up into a sitting position and manoeuvred myself down to my skis. They had frozen into the snow. But I got one of them loose and, when I had wiped the snow and ice off it, I began piercing the snow all about where I had been lying with the straight heel of it.

I thought I should never find that other stick. In desperation I tried lower down. And at last I located it, quite near the surface and close to the spot where my other ski still stood bedded in the snow. It must have been ripped from my hand as I went into the snow.

I lay down then. I had no more energy. My body felt chilled right through. Yet the blood glowed in my veins with the fever of exhaustion. But I was no longer helpless. I had both my sticks. Soon I should be on my skis again. Soon—when I had enough strength. All the warmth died out of me as I lay there. I began to feel cold and very sleepy. I thought about my skis. I had to get them on. It would be such a struggle. My thoughts were limited now to that one action. The world was condensed into a pair of skis.

I think I should have lain there, relaxed, until the snow drifted right over me, if I hadn't been lying for support across that one ski. I was lying with the full weight of my body on the toe stops and the sharp steel pressed painfully against my ribs.

At last I made a supreme effort of will and lifted myself off the ski. As I sat up, a pile of drift snow sifted off my body. The wind struck fresh on my face as it cleared the edges of the hole. It seemed lighter now. There was less snow falling. I looked at the up-ended haft of my other ski. It stood straight up, like a smooth slat of wood erected to mark the grave of a man who had died there.

Pressing with one hand on the free ski and the other on one of my sticks, I wriggled over to it. It was frozen tight. I had to work hard to loosen it. But at last it came out. Then I sat in the snow and cleared the ice from both skis and waxed them.

I did not stop now. I felt that, if I stopped to rest, I should never have the strength of will to rise again. I swivelled round so that I was lying slightly above my skis. I bedded them firmly into the snow and then cleaned the snow from my boots. But it was not easy to fix the skis to the boots. My fingers were stiff and they seemed to have no strength in them. And when at last I had the clips round the heels of my boots, the heavy spring clip in front of the toe seemed as though it had lost its spring. It took every last ounce of energy I possessed to pull those powerful clips over.

But at last it was done, and, as I lay panting there, I felt the comfort of the heavy skis on my feet. It is strange—when one comes fresh to skis after a long time, they seem so clumsy on one's feet. But, believe me, if you try to stand in soft snow without them, you feel as though you are trying to row without a boat. And it is a wonderful feeling to have your skis solid under your feet again.

After a little while, I took hold of my sticks and forced myself upright until I was crouched on my toes with the skis under me.

Then at last I rose to my feet and stood there in the snow, looking down at the trampled hole that I had torn with my body in the soft whiteness of the valley.

I could hardly stand for weariness and the cramped aching

of my cold limbs. But it was a wonderful sensation just to stand upright again, no longer in the clutches of the snow, but treading it firmly beneath my feet, able to move upon it. I felt like a man who has climbed a great peak and feels the whole world and the elements conquered.

Slowly I stamped my feet to restore the circulation. And whilst I was doing this, I began to consider what I should do. Where was Mayne? To go down to Carbonin was easiest. If I kept travelling downhill, I should strike the pass. But should I? All about me was a jumbled heap of snow hills. Mayne's tracks were completely obliterated. The snow drifted like a white sandstorm, a moving surf of powder clinging close to the lying snow. Mayne had probably led me off the beaten track. If I followed the valley down, it might only lead me farther into the mountains. And suppose I made the pass? Mayne had said it was narrow—so narrow that it was impossible to lose one's way. Suppose he was waiting for me in that pass? He would wait a long time. He would want to be sure. I looked quickly about me. At this very moment he might be standing on the edge of visibility, watching and waiting to pounce on me if I looked like getting out of this white jungle alive. I remembered what Keramikos had said of him.

As I looked about me, the wind suddenly changed. It began to blow down from the glacier. The snow and the leaden sky was swept slowly away like a gauze curtain being drawn back. Black peaks began to stand out above me. The snow hills all round me were no longer blurred shapes, but sharp and clearly defined. Ahead of me and about a thousand yards down the valley was a glacier. It was not the Cristallo glacier which we had crossed much higher up, but another and smaller glacier. Its black moraines showed quite clear against the snow. It was circled by ragged crests. There was no sign of a pass. There was also no sign of Mayne.

I was convinced then that he had led me off the proper track. This was borne out later when I had a chance to look at a map.

The small glacier that I was looking down on to was the one under Monte Cristallino. After crossing the main Cristallo glacier, Mayne had swung hard to the right, away from the pass to Carbonin.

It was that freak change in the weather that decided my course of action, and incidentally saved my life. If it had remained thick, I should have gone on down the valley to the Cristallino glacier. And there I should have frittered away my energy until nightfall. And that would have been the end.

But that sudden lifting of the snow showed me that there was only one thing to do; retrace my steps to the main Cristallo glacier, cross the top of the pass under Popena and go down to Col da Varda the way we had come up.

It was a big decision to make, for it meant climbing more than a thousand feet. And if the snow came down again and I lost my way, I knew I should not have a hope. But at least I knew there was a way through and, even if it began to snow again, I might remember the contours of the ground sufficiently to find my way back. To go forward meant facing the unknown and possibly Mayne. And though I would have been glad to go down instead of up, I dared not risk meeting Mayne. He was too good a ski-er. I should not have a chance.

So I turned and faced the long white slope down which I had come so easily and so fast. It took me two hours by my watch to climb that slope. I had to go slowly, with many halts, zig-zagging up in a series of gentle diagonals. It was past two by the time I reached the top and looked down on to a grey sea of cloud out of which distant peaks rose like islands. The snow had cleared from the mountain tops and lay like a dirty blanket on their slopes, filling the great valley fissures.

I will not record the details of that journey. There were times when I stood, my head bowed on my sticks, certain I could not go another yard. On these occasions, it was only by the greatest exercise of my will that I prevented my knees from folding under the weight of my body. All I desired was to relax and sleep. Once

I was careless and fell. The muscles of my arms and legs barely had the strength to thrust me back on to the skis again. And, of course, the higher I climbed, the weaker I became, owing to the altitude.

The glacier seemed interminable. Twice, as I struggled across it, snow came down in a grey curtain from Monte Cristallo. But each time it drifted on, down into the valleys. The incline was gentle enough here. But, though my skis slipped easily through the powdery snow, it was a real effort to drag each ski forward. I used my sticks. But there seemed no strength in the thrust of my arms. The wind cut into my wet clothing and froze it, so that, despite my exertions, it became stiff and unyielding and as cold as the snow itself.

At length I reached the place where the smooth rock outcropped and took my skis off. Across my shoulders they were a dead weight. They cut into my shoulders and weighed me down so that I staggered rather than walked.

But at length I stood at the very top of the pass. The air was white—translucent with light as it had been when we had passed this point nearly five hours ago. The peak of Popena stood up, cold and black, and all around me was that world of angry-looking crests. The wind came up from Col da Varda with a violence that whipped the snow away from under my very feet. Everything was just as it had been before, except that Mayne was no longer with me.

I stumbled on from outcrop to outcrop until I stood on the rim of that white basin out of which we had climbed. I set my skis up-ended in a drift and stared unhappily at that frightening slope. The tracks we had made were still there, a line of hachures that rose to meet me out of the grey murk of snow that filled the lower reaches of the pass. The ski marks were faint and dusted with snow. But they were still visible, like a friendly signpost, marking the way back to warmth and safe sleep.

I put on my skis again and then, very slowly, began the descent, side-stepping down into grey cotton-wool clouds of snow. I kept my eyes on my feet. Once and once only was I fool enough to look down the line of the faint ski marks I was following. They seemed to fall away from under my skis and my knees became weak and trembled, so that I dared not make the next step down for fear the upper ski would slip. It took me ten minutes, or thereabouts, to nerve myself to continue. After that I kept my eyes on my skis. My exhaustion was so great that I found difficulty in placing my skis properly and several times one or other of my skis began to slide from under me.

But I made it in the end. And it was a great relief to see the ski points sizzling through the snow of their own accord like the prows of two ships, thrusting the powdered snow back on either side. I felt safe then, even though the leaden grey cloud mist closed about me and the snow began to blow into my face.

I must have been about halfway down the pass, when figures loomed out of the driving snow. There were several of them. I forget how many. But I saw Joe's heavy bulk among them. I hullooed to them and waved one of my sticks. They stopped. I made straight for them, the snow fairly melting under my skis. They seemed to come towards me very fast out of a blur of snow. I remember seeing Joe crouch down, training his baby camera on me. Then the blur became a blank. Apparently I just fell unconscious in my tracks.

When I came to, rough hands were chafing at my legs and arms. I was lying on the snow and Joe was bending over me. The cold rim of a flask touched my lips and I nearly choked with the fire of brandy in my throat. Somebody had taken off my skis and a blanket had been spread over me.

'What happened?' Joe asked.

'Mayne,' I gasped. 'Tried to—murder me.' I closed my eyes. I felt so tired.

As if from a great distance, I heard Joe's voice say, 'Must be delirious.'

An Italian began talking. I could not hear what he was saying. I was only half-conscious. I wished they would go away and let me sleep. Then I was hoisted on to somebody's back and the wind was cold on my face again. That and the strain on my arms brought me to full consciousness. My cheek touched dark, thick-growing hair under a peaked cap. Out of the corner of my eyes I could see dark tufts growing in a man's ear. My direct line of vision was towards the points of his skis pushing fast through the dry snow. He was ski-ing without sticks, his arms under my knees and his hands locked in mine. It was a pretty frightening way to travel, though I learned later that he was one of the guides from Tre Croci and had often carried casualties in that manner down the mountains.

'I think I'll be all right now,' I told him in Italian.

'You will faint,' he said. 'You are too weak.'

But I insisted and at length he stopped and set me down. They fixed my skis for me and then, with the guide travelling beside me, I continued under my own steam. He was quite right. I did feel faint and terribly weak. But, having said I could make it, I was determined to do so.

But I was very glad to see the snow-covered gables of Col da Varda. It seemed like coming home after a long journey. The guide and Joe helped me up to my room. Between them they got my clothes off and then started to massage my body to bring back the circulation. The pain in my hands and feet was indescribable as the blood returned to half-frozen veins. Then I was put to bed with hot-water bottles that Anna brought up, and I fell immediately into a deep sleep.

I woke to find Joe standing beside me with a tray of food. 'It's past ten,' he said. 'You've slept for nearly four hours. Better have some food now.' I sat up then. I felt much better; very stiff, but quite fit.

Joe went to the door. 'Come in,' he said. 'He's awake.'

It was Mayne who entered. 'My God, Blair!' he said. 'I'm glad to see you.' He sat down uninvited at the foot of the bed. 'I've only just got back from Carbonin. I was in despair when we were searching up through the pass. We couldn't find a trace of you. Then, when we got back at nightfall, there was Wesson's message saying they'd picked you up on this side. I've never been so glad to get a telephone message. I'd almost given up hope. How do you feel? What happened?'

It was incredible. That charming, boyish smile. It was so natural. But it did not extend to the eyes. Those grey eyes of his were expressionless. They told me nothing. Or was that my imagination? He seemed so delighted to see me. He made it sound important to him that I was alive. But all I could think of was that wall of snow rushing up to meet me and the great swirl of snow where he'd Christied into the floor of the valley. 'You should know what happened,' I said coldly. 'You meant it to happen.'

He went on as though he had not understood my remark. 'When I got to the end of that valley, I found I was on the edge of a glacier. It was the Cristallino Glacier. I knew then, of course, that we had struck much too far to the right. I waited there for a few minutes. When you didn't show up, I began to get worried. I started back up my ski tracks. But I hadn't realised how quickly the snow was covering up my tracks. By the time I'd gone back five hundred yards, there was no trace of them left. The valley wasn't clearly defined. Without any tracks to guide me, there were innumerable ways I might have come down. The snow had been so thick in my face that I could not remember the features of the ground. It was a maze of little valleys. I tramped up every one I could find. I climbed from one to the other, calling to you. And in the end I thought you must have had a spill, found my tracks covered and made your own way. I went on down to Carbonin then, and when I found you hadn't arrived I telephoned here for them to send out a search-party from this end, and then started back up the pass with all the decent ski-ers I could muster at the Carbonin Hotel. My God!' he said with an apologetic smile, 'I don't think I've ever been so scared. You see, I felt it was my fault. I should have realised that my tracks were being covered up like that and kept closer touch with you. What did happen?' he asked.

I was staggered at his nerve. 'You mean to say you've really no idea what happened?' I demanded angrily. 'Christ! You've got a nerve, Mayne.' I was trembling. 'Why did you take that steep slope as a direct run? You had to Christi at the bottom to avoid the soft snow on the other side of the valley. And you knew I couldn't Christi.'

'But I didn't Christi,' he said, and looked me straight in the eyes, perfectly cool. 'There was quite a nice banking turn at the bottom. I took it as a straight turn. I know it was a bit fast, but there was nothing difficult about it. I certainly didn't have to Christi.'

'That's a lie,' I said.

He gazed at me in astonishment. 'I repeat: I did not have to Christi. You'd made out so well, I thought you'd take that bit in your stride.'

'You know very well I couldn't take it in my stride.' I felt calmer now. 'You had to Christi and you knew I was bound to crash into that soft snow.'

'Oh, for God's sake!' he said. 'What are you trying to prove?'

I looked at him for a moment. Could I have been mistaken? But that swirl of torn-up snow in the bottom of that valley—the picture of it was so clear in my mind. I said, 'Mind if I ask you a question?'

'Of course not.'

'You joined the Army in 1942. What happened to you after you landed in Italy?'

He looked puzzled. 'I don't get what you're driving at, Blair,' he said. 'I joined the Army in 1940, not 1942. Went overseas in '43—North Africa. I was a troop commander in an Ack-Ack Regiment. We landed at Salerno. I was taken prisoner, escaped and then joined UNRRA and went to Greece. But what's that got to do with—?'

'Forget it,' I said. 'I'm a bit strung-up, that's all.' And I lay back against the pillow.

'Well, anyway,' he said, 'I'm glad you're all right. I did everything I could. I'm terribly sorry about it. It was my fault. I realise that. But I honestly thought you'd have no difficulty at the bottom of that run. I blame myself for not realising that the tracks were being covered up so quickly.' He got up then.

I said, 'Don't worry about it.'

When he had gone out of the room, Joe uncovered a plate of scrambled eggs and placed it beside me. 'What the devil were you driving at, Neil?' he asked as I began to eat. 'Why question him about his Army career?'

'Because somebody told me he was a deserter,' I said, with my mouth full. It was good to taste food again. 'One of them is a liar. I'll find out which before I'm through.'

'Don't understand your attitude,' he grunted. 'Mayne's a decent enough fellow. He couldn't have done more. Rang us up as soon as he got into Carbonin. I answered the phone. He was terribly worried. He must have been dog-tired after a bad run like that. But he went straight out again with a search-party he got together at Carbonin. Didn't get in till dark. It wasn't his fault he couldn't locate you.'

I shrugged my shoulders and went on eating. He seemed to be annoyed by my silence. 'I think you're being damned uncharitable in the matter,' he went on. 'Know what you said when you came to and I was giving you brandy? I asked what had happened. And you told me that Mayne had tried to murder you.'

I looked up at his heavy, friendly features. He was so sure of the world about him. It was just something to take pictures of. 'You thought I was just unstrung by what had happened?'

'Of course you were,' he said soothingly. 'Believe me, that boy did all he could. It wasn't his fault that you went into some soft snow and that his ski tracks got covered up. Anything can happen up in the mountains when it comes on thick like that. The guide who carried you part of the way down, he told me several stories of people caught that way. Trouble was you tried to do too much when you were out of practice.'

I said nothing after that. What was the good? But Mayne had lied when he said he'd done a straight turn at the bottom of that run.

Joe left me then and I lay in bed, comfortably relaxed. I tried to read. But I could not concentrate. In the end, I put the book down and just lay there, trying to get things clear in my mind.

It must have been about an hour later that Joe came in. 'Engles wants you on the phone,' he said. 'He's down at the Splendido. Says he tried to contact you earlier, but couldn't get any sense out of Aldo. I told him you oughtn't to be disturbed, but he was insistent. You know what he's like,' he added apologetically. 'If you were dying, he'd still want me to rout you out. I tried to tell him what had happened. But he wouldn't listen. Never will listen to anything in which he doesn't figure. Do you feel like coming down, or shall I tell him to go to hell?'

'No, I'll come,' I said. I got out of bed and slipped a blanket round my shoulders over my dressing-gown.

'Wonder what he's come over for,' Joe said as he followed me out of the door. My knees felt a bit weak and stiff. Otherwise I seemed all right. 'Why the devil doesn't he leave us to get on with it on our own?' he grumbled behind me. 'It's always the same. Feels he isn't doing his job unless he's goading everybody on. Have you got a synopsis for him?'

'I haven't done too badly,' I said. But I was thinking of Engles' private mission, not of the script.

The telephone was on the bar, by the coffee geyser. Mayne and Valdini looked up as I came in. They were seated by the stove. Valdini said, 'You feel better, Mr Blair? I am glad. I was afraid for you when I heard you had mislaid your way.'

'I feel fine now, thanks,' I replied.

I picked up the receiver. 'That you, Neil?' Engles' voice sounded thin over the wire. 'What's all this Wesson was saying about an accident?'

I was conscious that both Mayne and Valdini were watching me and listening to the conversation. 'I don't think it was quite that,' I replied. 'Tell you about it tomorrow. Are you coming up?'

'Snow's pretty thick down here,' came the reply. 'But I'll be up if I have to come through on skis. I've booked a room. You might see that it's laid on. What have you discovered about Mayne—anything?'

'Look,' I said. 'I can't tell you the plot now. This telephone is in the bar. Give you a full synopsis when I see you.'

'I get you. But I think I've recognised him from those pictures you sent. Had the roll developed the instant it arrived. It was that scar that gave me the clue. That's why I flew over. Watch him, Neil. If he's the bloke I think he is, he's a dangerous customer. By the way, I've got that little bitch, Carla, with me. She's had ten Martinis and is now telling me I'm nice and not a bit English. We'll see if our impressions of her so beautiful nature tally—yes?' He gave a quick laugh. 'See you tomorrow, then.' And he rang off.

Joe thrust a drink across to me as I put down the phone. 'Everything all right?' he asked.

'Seems to be,' I said.

'What's he come over for? Did he tell you?'

'Oh, I think he just wants to look over the ground for himself,' I replied.

'He would. Still, he's a bloody good director. Queer fellow. Mother was Welsh, you know. That's where he gets that love of music and that flashy brilliance of speech and intellect. They're all the same, the Welsh—flashy, superficial, no depth to them.'

'There's a bit more to him than that,' I said.

'Well, he's not all Welsh, that's why. Don't know what his father was—something dour, probably a Scot. That's what makes him so moody and gives him that dogged seeking after perfection. Two sides of his nature always at war with each other. Makes him difficult to work with. Still, it's his strength as a director.'

I finished my drink and went back to bed. Joe fussed after me like a mother—had my hot-water bottles refilled, put a bottle of cognac beside my bed and saw to it that I had some cigarettes. 'Want me to kiss you good-night?' he asked with a grin.

'I think I can get along without that,' I laughed.

'Okay,' he said and switched out the light. 'You'll feel fine tomorrow.'

As soon as his footsteps had died away, I got up and locked the door. I was taking no chances.

I had not been in the warmth of my bed more than a few minutes before ski boots clattered along the bare boards of the corridor and there was a knock at the door. 'Who's there?' I asked.

'Keramikos,' was the reply.

'Just a minute,' I said. I slipped out of bed and unlocked the door. Then I put the light on and hopped back into bed. 'Come in,' I called.

He entered and shut the door. He stood for a moment at the foot of my bed, looking at me. It was difficult to see the expression of his eyes behind those thick lenses. They reflected the light and looked like two round white discs. 'So,' he said, 'it was not the *slittovia*, eh?'

'How do you mean?' I asked. But I understood.

He ignored my question. 'You lock your door now, hm? You are learning.'

'You're not surprised that I had an accident whilst out with Mayne, are you?' I said.

'I am never surprised at anything, my friend,' he replied evasively.

I tried another line. 'You told me Mayne was a deserter and that he joined the Army in 1942. He says he joined in 1940.'

'He's probably right, then. I don't know Gilbert Mayne's history. I only know this man's history.'

'Are you suggesting that this is not the real Gilbert Mayne?' I asked, for I did not know what other interpretation to put on his words.

He shrugged his shoulders. 'Perhaps,' he said. 'But I did not come to discuss Mayne with you. I felt it would be courteous, as a fellow-guest, Mr Blair, to come and offer you my felicitations on your narrow escape. Wesson tells me the director of your film company has arrived. Will he be staying here?'

'For a few days,' I told him. 'He should interest you. He was in Greece for a time.'

'Greece?' He seemed interested. 'In the Army?'

'Yes,' I said. 'Intelligence.'

He gave me a quick look. 'Then perhaps he and I will have much to talk about?'

He bade me good-night then. But as he reached the door I said, 'By the way, when you examine what is written on a sheet of typing paper in the machine, you should always see that it is rolled back to the original position.'

'I do not follow,' he said.

'You searched my room last night,' I reminded him.

He looked at me hard. Then he said, 'Whoever searched your room, Mr Blair, it was not me—that I assure you.' And he closed the door. I at once got up and locked it.

6

An Ugly Scene

When I looked out of my window next morning it was a different world. There was no sunshine, no sharp contrast between black and white. The sky was grey with falling snow—large flakes that moved slowly downwards in their millions. The ground was a dull blanket of white. The trees were so laden with snow that they scarcely seemed trees at all. The belvedere was no longer a platform of bare boards. It was a square of virgin white, the round table-tops bulging with snow like giant mushrooms.

I felt quite all right—just tired and very stiff. I went downstairs and phoned Emilio at the bottom of the *slittovia*. He told me that the sleigh could make it at the moment, but that if the wind rose and the snow began to drift, it would not be possible. I then phoned the Splendido and left a message for Engles that if he could get through to Tre Croci, the *slittovia* would be able to bring him up to Col da Varda. Then I told Aldo to prepare the remaining room.

I suppose I should now switch straight to Engles' arrival at Col da Varda, for nothing happened until after he had arrived. But, since everything hinged on that event, I must give some account of the strange air of expectancy that pervaded the bar room that morning.

In the case of Joe and myself it was understandable. Joe was mentally preparing himself for a verbal clash with his director. 'Engles will be full of ideas, damn his eyes,' he grumbled to me. 'But a film's got to have a focal point, and the focal point, as I see it, is this hut and the *slittovia*. It's a terrific setting. Look at it this morning! Another few hours and we'll be snowbound up here. What a situation for, say, a group of people who hate each other, or whose interests clash!' This was said to me at breakfast, and the others listened to his words with peculiar attention. 'And the *slittovia*,' he added. 'I've got some fine shots of it. Rig up a dummy sleigh and have it hurtle down with the cable broken. And a ski chase—I've got a wonderful shot of you, Neil, as you came down that pass and collapsed at our feet. If Engles doesn't agree with me—damn it, I'll resign.'

Joe was strung up and marshalling his points. And for myself, I must admit to a sense of excitement. After all that had happened, I felt certain Engles must tell me why he had sent me out here.

But the others—why were they so silent? Mayne had greeted me cheerfully enough when he came in to breakfast. He asked me how I felt with the quiet solicitude of a friend who was glad to see me none the worse for an unfortunate mishap. He was charming and natural, but quieter than usual. Anna's big eyes smiled at him unanswered as she laid the table. And when Joe came down and began to talk of Engles' arrival, he fell strangely silent.

And Valdini, who could have talked out any bill had he been an American senator, said hardly a word. Joe noticed it and said, 'What's on your mind, Valdini. In trouble with that contessa of yours?'

'Always you make the fun of me, Wesson, eh?' snarled the little Sicilian.

'Well, you looked damned worried when she phoned you last night,' Joe replied.

'When was that?' I asked.

'Oh, after you'd finally gone to bed,' Joe answered.

So she had phoned him after Engles had spoken to me. I would have given much to have known what she had said. That it concerned Engles I had no doubt.

And Keramikos. He was always quiet and reserved. But this morning he appeared not so much reserved as watchful. He regarded the breakfast-table with amused detachment. And yet there was a trace of nervousness in his manner. It seems quite natural for him to have been nervous now that I know the whole story. But at the time it was strange, because he always had such an air of confidence.

After breakfast everyone huddled round the stove. And that was strange, too, because normally they all drifted off to their rooms.

Joe talked to me for a time about the film. He wanted my support. He tried to get me to give him a synopsis of the script I was supposed to have planned. Was I using the hut and the *slittovia*? What snow scenes had I planned? And when he found me uncommunicative, he too fell silent. Finally he confirmed my feeling that the atmosphere was tense. 'Seems this snow has the same effect on people as the *mistral* or the *sirocco*. How long is it likely to last, Mayne?'

'A day or two maybe,' Mayne replied.

'My God!' Joe said. 'Are we going to sit as glum as owls round this stove for several days? For the love of God, Mayne, get on that piano and hammer out something cheerful. Can't say I usually like the row you kick up in the mornings. But anything is better than the five of us brooding over this monstrosity of a stove.'

But Mayne said he did not feel in the mood. And nobody supported Joe in his demand for music. In the end, he went and got a book. But even with one of his inevitable Westerns, his mind did not seem able to settle down. Valdini sat picking his teeth with a match. Mayne and Keramikos seemed lost in thought.

So we waited. And at last, about ten-thirty, the drone of the cable told us that the sleigh was coming up. Nobody moved. But the atmosphere quickened to interest. I got up and went over to the window that looked out on to the sleigh track. 'Who's coming up—your director?' Mayne asked.

'Can't see yet,' I told him. Visibility was very poor. The sleigh track lost itself in the grey murk of falling snow.

Mayne came over and stood beside me. The cable jerked clear

of the snow. And then, like a ghost ship, the sleigh emerged from the snow. 'Looks as though there are two passengers on it,' he said. 'Who else would want to come up on a day like this?' He swung round. 'Do you know who the other passenger is, Valdini?'

The little man looked up from the contemplation of his fingernails. He was dressed in a suit of sky blue with a dark-blue shirt and a crimson tie. He looked like the leader of a hot rhythm outfit. His rubber face grinned. But the grin did not extend to the eyes, which were watchful and narrowed. He sucked at his teeth. 'It is possible,' he said.

The sleigh was nearing the top now. It was thick with snow. I recognised the two passengers seated behind Emilio—they were Engles and the Contessa.

The sleigh stopped at the little wooden platform, which was almost under the window. Engles looked up, saw me and nodded a brief greeting. Mayne took a quick breath and then walked casually back to the stove. Carla was talking gaily to Engles as they got their skis off the rack on the sleigh. Anna went out and took Engles' two suitcases.

I turned back into the room. The others were seated exactly as they had been before. Nobody spoke. The ticking of the cuckoo clock was quite loud. I went over to the bar and got out a bottle of cognac and some glasses. There was a clatter of skis being placed against the wooden walls of the hut. Then the door opened and the Contessa came in, followed by Engles. Joe got up and said, 'Hallo, Engles. Glad to see you. Had a good trip?' That was the only movement from the group by the stove. Mayne and Keramikos were watching Engles, and Valdini was watching the Contessa.

Joe sensed the silence and tried to talk it down. 'Here, I'll put your coat on the table. Need a drink, I expect, old man. Ah, I see Neil has already had the same idea. Well, better introduce you since you're staying here. We're all present. Can't get out in this damned snow.'

Engles nodded briefly at the group by the stove as Joe introduced him. Then he said, 'Come and have a drink, Joe. I want to hear what sort of shots you've got for me. You need a drink, too, Carla. What are you having?'

She removed her heavy fur-lined jacket. She was dressed in her scarlet ski-suit. It was a pleasant splash of colour in that drab room. 'I would like a *strega*, please, Derek.' And she took his arm as though he were the one man in the world.

Engles gave me a quick, secret smile. I poured the drinks. Joe began talking about his focal point. Engles was only half-listening. His attention kept wandering to a battered mirror that hung on the wall at the end of the bar. At first I thought he was checking up on his appearance. He was always meticulous about his toilet when women were around. But then I realised that he could not possibly see himself in it. What he could see was the little group by the fire.

I switched my attention and saw that Mayne, too, was watching that little mirror. Joe rambled on about the importance of the *slittovia* from the camera point of view. Engles did not even pretend to be interested. He was watching Mayne and there was something between amusement and excitement in his dark eyes.

At last Mayne got up and came over to the bar. His movements were casual enough, but it was a deliberate casualness. He and Engles were much of a height when they stood together, though Engles seemed shorter because of the slight stoop of his shoulders. Joe paused for breath and Mayne said, 'As you're joining us in this hermit's existence up here, Mr Engles, perhaps you will have a drink with me?'

'I'd like to,' Engles replied.

Mayne poured the drinks, chalked himself up for the round, brought Keramikos and Valdini in and, in short, became a most charming and natural host, talking pleasantly and easily of the advantages of peacetime air travel as compared with conditions in wartime. 'But peace or war,' he said, 'I can never reconcile

myself to the take-off—that uninsurable half-minute when your
eyes won't focus on your book and you feel hot and there is
that rattling roar of the engines as the ground rushes past the
window faster and faster and then suddenly recedes.'

Joe, who had been content to pause for another drink, now
dived back into the original conversation. 'There's one point at
any rate, Engles,' he said, 'that I'd like to get settled before I take
any more shots. Do we or do we not—?'

'I don't think you'll be doing much camera work for some
little time,' Mayne interrupted him. 'Look at it now!'

He was pointing at the window and we all turned. Outside,
it had suddenly become even darker. The snow was lifting up
before it reached the ground and swirling round in eddies. Then,
suddenly, all those millions of little jostling snowflakes seemed to
fall into order of battle and charge against the trees on the far
side of the *slittovia*. The whole hut shook with that first gust of
wind. It whined and ramped round the gables as though intent
upon plucking the hut off Col da Varda and whirling it away
into space. It took hold of the trees and shook them like a terrier
shakes a rat. The snow fell in great slabs from their whipping
branches. A wave of snow swept up from the ground and flung
itself across the sleigh track. Then the wind steadied down to a
hard blow, driving the snowflakes almost horizontal to the ground.

'Looks as though you'll have to spend the night up here,
Carla,' Engles said.

She smiled. 'Will you be a nice man, then, and give up your
room for me?'

'Do not be afraid, Mr Engles,' Valdini said with a horrid leer.
'She has so kind a nature—she will not insist that you sleep
down here.'

There was an awkward silence which Carla broke with a
laugh. 'Do not mind Stefan,' she said to Engles. 'He is jealous,
that is all.'

'Jealous!' Valdini's eyes hardened and he looked at Mayne. 'Yes,

I am jealous. Do you know what it is like to be jealous, Mr Mayne?' His voice was dangerously suave and once again I had that feeling of unpleasant emotions kept just below the surface.

The hut shook to a renewed onslaught of the wind. It thrashed through the tops of the firs, tearing from them their last remnants of snow so that they stood up, black and bare, in that grey, white-speckled world.

'Lucky we're not on that glacier now, eh, Blair?' Mayne said to me. Then to Engles: 'You know you nearly lost your script writer yesterday?'

'I heard he'd had an accident ski-ing,' Engles replied. 'What happened?'

Mayne gave his version. He told it well and I listened with some admiration. Engles could hear what really happened later. 'It was just of one those things,' Mayne concluded. 'My fault, really. I should have kept closer touch.'

'What happened to you?' Engles asked, turning to me. 'You had a spill in soft snow, I suppose. Did you get back on your own?'

I told him how a freak change in the weather had enabled me to get back across the glacier and how a search-party had picked me up half-way down the pass.

'I've got a shot of him collapsing as he reached us,' Joe said. 'It's a real beauty. You want a scene like that in the script. It'll grip any audience. His companion telephoning from an hotel, search-parties starting out, the man himself struggling out of the soft snow, trekking back over the pass, and finally collapsing. Have his girl with the rescue party.'

Engles seemed lost in thought for a moment. Then his eyes lighted up with that infectious enthusiasm. 'That's wasting it, Joe. You can get more drama into it than that. And to hell with the girl. Listen—suppose Mayne here wanted to murder Blair. He's a good ski-er. Blair isn't. A snowstorm comes up. Mayne's leading. He bears right after crossing the glacier—not by mistake, but by design.' I scarcely heard what he said after that. I was watching Mayne. At the mention of 'murder' he had stiffened. He glanced quickly at Keramikos. His eyes were blank and he passed his tongue once or twice across his lips.

'A night out there in a storm, and he's bound to freeze to death,' I heard Engles saying. 'The perfect murder. Can't be proved. But, by a freak chance, Blair comes back. It's a lovely situation. We'll write that into the script, Neil,' he added, turning to me.

Keramikos thrust his head forward. 'This hypothetical case,' he said. 'It is most interesting. But why should Mayne wish to kill Blair?'

'Ah! That is what we have to work out,' Engles said. Then he turned to me. 'Come on, Neil,' he said. 'We'll get this down whilst the idea is clear in our minds. Where can we go? What about your room? Any heating?'

'There's an electric stove,' I said.

'Good!'

As soon as we were outside the door I said, 'Whatever induced you to produce that murder idea?'

'Well, it wasn't a bad idea,' he said, grinning up at me as we mounted the stairs.

'No,' I said. 'It wasn't at all a bad idea. In fact, it's exactly what happened. Mayne tried to murder me.'

'Yes, I guessed as much.'

'How could you?' I said. We were in my room now.

'Your unwillingness to talk on the phone. And what I know of Mayne.'

I shut the door and switched on the electric heater. It was very cold and the snow was piling up against the window, so that it was almost impossible to see out. 'What do you know of Mayne?' I asked.

He gave me a quick glance as he seated himself on the bed and produced a packet of cigarettes. 'That can wait for the moment, Neil. Let's hear what's been happening up here. The last message I got from you was the cable giving details of the auction. It was that and the photograph of the bunch downstairs that brought me over here. Let's start with the auction.'

When I had given him a full description of the sale, he asked me to give him all the information on Mayne, Keramikos, Valdini and Carla. I started with Carla. I told him all that she had told me about herself. 'And you believed her?' he cut in.

'I saw no reason not to,' I replied. 'She's pretty sensual, but that's no reason why she shouldn't really have been in love with Stelben.'

He gave a cynical laugh. 'That woman in love! She's never loved any one but herself. She's clever and she can handle men. She's twisted you round her little finger, Neil.'

'Don't be ridiculous,' I said angrily. 'It's a perfectly reasonable story.'

'Reasonable!' He laughed outright. 'It's about as reasonable as a tiger migrating to the Antarctic. What use would that woman have for a secluded villa on top of Col da Varda? She has two interests only in life—and money is the chief one. The trouble with you, Neil, is that you know nothing about women and are as gullible as any man I have ever met.'

I shrugged my shoulders. 'Have it your own way,' I said. 'But do you expect me to have second sight? How should I know whether she's telling the truth or not? Suppose you give me all the information you have about these people. Then I'd have something to go on.'

He smiled. 'All right, Neil—a fair point. That's Carla and Valdini. What about Keramikos?'

I told him what Keramikos had said of Mayne, of the meeting in the *slittovia* machine-room and how the Greek had denied that he had searched my room.

'Anything on Mayne?' he asked after that.

'Only what Keramikos told me, and then that ski trip yesterday.'

He considered for a moment. 'You haven't done badly at all, Neil,' he said with a sudden friendly smile. Again he paused.

106

Then he said, 'Suppose it was Mayne who searched your room that night? Would that have given him grounds for wanting to get rid of you?'

'Hardly,' I said. And then I remembered the sheet of typescript in my typewriter. 'Yes, it might,' I added. 'I'd written a report for you. It was an account of what Keramikos had told me. Whoever it was who searched my rooms had had a look at that.'

He nodded. 'And suppose the man that Keramikos had talked with that night was Mayne? Could it have been Mayne?'

'I don't know,' I replied. 'I didn't really see him. But he was tall enough. It could have been.'

'And if it was, then Mayne would have drawn certain conclusions from the fact that you were not in your room. Yes. I think it must have been our friend Mayne.'

There was a pause then. He seemed to have come to the end of his questions. 'Look,' I said. 'It's about time you gave me some idea of what's going on here.'

He considered the point. Then he said, 'You'll be surprised at this, Neil. I know less than you do really. I know the background of Mayne and the Greek. But I don't know how they fit into the Carla-Valdini set-up. There's tension there, I can see that. But why? No, the only thing I know that you don't is the reason they're all here. And the less you know about that the safer you'll be. I don't think you're in any real danger now that I've arrived. For the rest, I think it will all resolve itself—with a little help. This place is just about snowbound. Everybody who is interested in Col da Varda is cooped up inside this hut.' He laughed and there was a devil of excitement lurking in his dark eyes. 'We'll have some fun now. The pot is ready to boil over. We'll go down and start stoking up the fires. Whatever I say, or whatever I do, Neil—don't interfere. Just keep in the background and watch the fireworks.' He got up abruptly then and opened the door. 'And don't say anything to old Wesson about this. All his thrills are on celluloid. If he met one in real life, he'd have a fit.'

107

When we returned to the bar, only Carla and Mayne were there. Carla was still drinking *strega* and, judging by the flush on her cheeks, she had had quite a number whilst we had been out of the room. Mayne had recovered his ease of manner on cognac. Aldo was behind the bar. '*Due cognaci*,' Engles ordered.

'*Si, si—subito, signore.*'

'Where's Wesson?' Engles asked Mayne.

'Gone to develop some negatives for you.'

'And Valdini and the Greek?'

'They have gone to see him develop,' Carla answered. 'But why Stefan is interested when he knows the pictures are not pornographic, I do not know,' she added with a laugh.

Mayne was watching Engles—watching and waiting for him. The tension between them was uncomfortable. Engles drank in silence for a moment. Carla said nothing. She watched the two of them, and there was a gleam in her eye that I did not understand.

It was Mayne who made the first move. I don't think he could stand that silence. 'Have you thought out why I should want to kill Blair?' he asked. He tried to make his voice sound casual, but the tremor in it betrayed tense nerves.

Engles looked at him. Then he turned to Carla. 'You remember last night, when you told me what Mayne really was—you said he had double-crossed you?'

Carla nodded, and her eyes gleamed like those of a cat in the dark. Mayne set down his drink. His hand clenched as though about to hit out.

'Would it interest you to know,' Engles continued smoothly, 'that he is not content with double-crossing you—he plans to murder you?'

'That's a lie!' Mayne cried. Then with a sneer to cover that too emphatic denial, 'And how was I supposed to be planning to kill Carla?'

Engles smiled. But he still addressed Carla and not Mayne.

'The *slittovia*. A loosened cog and an accident—and that was to be the end of you, Carla, and Valdini.'

'You must be mad,' Mayne said, his lips white. 'First it's Blair. And now Carla—and Valdini.' Then, in a quieter tone: 'I can't believe you're serious.'

'But I am serious,' Engles replied slowly. Then he suddenly leaned forward. It was as though he had pounced on the man. 'That affair yesterday was as much attempted murder, Mayne, as if you had pulled a knife and tried to slit Blair's throat.'

Mayne laughed. The laugh was pitched a shade too high. 'Try and prove that. My God, Engles, if this were England, I'd sue you for slander.'

'If this were England, my boy,' Engles replied, 'you'd be in a condemned cell awaiting execution.'

Mayne suddenly shrugged his shoulders. 'I think you must be mad,' he said and poured himself another drink. The scene might have ended there, for I think Engles would have regarded it as sufficient stoking of the fires for the time being. But then Carla suddenly stepped in. 'Gilbert,' she said, and her voice was silky soft like a panther padding to the kill, 'why did you wish to keel me?'

Mayne took his drink at a gulp and said, 'How should I know? Ask Engles. It's his fairy tale. Maybe he can tell you.'

'Perhaps I don't need to ask him.' The voice was purring, but I felt it was purring with hate. 'Perhaps I know.' The words came like the final crash of a chord.

Mayne was watchful now, his pale eyes cold and slightly narrowed. 'And why should I want to kill you?' he asked smoothly.

'Because I am no longer of use to you and I know too much.' Her voice was raised now. It was angry and bitter. 'You tried first to blackmail Heinrich. And when he would not tell you where it was hidden, you had him arrested. You dirty little *informante*! You killed my poor Heinrich.'

'Your poor Heinrich! You hated him. And he despised you.'

'That is not true,' she flared. 'He loved me—always.'

Mayne laughed. 'Loved you! He despised you. He kept you because you were useful to him. He was a fugitive in a foreign country, and you knew how to hide him. And you stayed with him because your greedy little soul was in love with a million in gold.'

'Greed! You talk about greed! You . . .'

Mayne went on drinking and allowed the flood of Italian invective to pass over his head. His manner was one of studied insolence. Carla suddenly stopped. There was a wild look in her eyes. 'I hate you,' she stormed. 'Do you hear? I hate you.'

'Do you, Carla?' He laughed. 'And it was such a short time ago that you were telling me you loved me. Don't you still love me?'

His supercilious, jeering voice seemed to hurt her. 'Why did you leave me, Gilbert?' Her voice was suddenly desperately quiet. 'We might have been very happy. Why did you leave me?'

'Because, as you very rightly guessed, you were no longer useful to me,' he answered coldly. 'You don't even know where the gold is, do you, Carla? Your poor Heinrich, who loved you so much, never told you. He killed a lot of men to get that gold. He shot them and buried them up here. After taking all that trouble, he wasn't going to tell his secret to a little prostitute he'd picked up in a Milan dance hall.'

'You—' With a quick movement of her wrist, Carla broke her tumbler against the brass rim of the bar and slashed at him with the broken edge.

It all happened in a flash. But even so, Mayne was quicker. He caught her wrist as she jabbed at his face and twisted it so that she spun round on her heels. He held her there, with her body arched in agony and her left hand clawing for his face with her blood-red nails.

It was at that moment that Valdini and Keramikos returned to the bar. I do not recall seeing Valdini get that gun out. It was a practised movement and very quick. I saw him come in out of the tail of my eye. He came in behind Keramikos. And, like the Greek, he stopped dead at the strange scene by the bar. Carla called to him something in Italian—or it may have been Sicilian, for I did not understand it. And in the same instant Valdini had that little black automatic in his hand.

'Keep very still, please, gentlemen,' he said, and his suave voice had an authoritative snap in it that went with the gun. 'I am a very good shot. Nobody move, please. Release the Contessa, Mr Mayne!'

Mayne let Carla's wrist go and she fell to the floor. She got to her feet in a single quick movement and picked up the broken tumbler. As her hands closed on the jagged remnant, she looked at Mayne. Her face was disfigured with rage. Her teeth were literally bared and her eyes smouldered. There was no doubt in our minds what she intended to do with that broken tumbler. She went slowly towards Mayne, her movements deliberate and sinuous. Mayne's jaw, where the scar showed, twitched nervously and he swallowed twice. There was nothing any of us could do. There had been something about Valdini's manner that had convinced us that he would not hesitate to shoot.

And it was at that moment that Joe came quietly in. He was looking at some negatives he had in his hand. The first he saw of the scene was the gun in Valdini's hand. 'Good God!' he said. 'You shouldn't point a gun at people like that. Might go off. Let's see if it's loaded.' And he stretched out his big hand and took the gun away from Valdini.

We did not move. We were so surprised. And the most surprised of all was Valdini. I know it sounds incredible. But that, I assure you, is exactly what happened. Joe Wesson walked in and took the gun out of Valdini's hand. And Valdini let him. The only explanation is that Joe had no fear. It never occurred to him that Valdini was prepared to shoot. And because he had no fear, Valdini lost his confidence.

Joe pulled out the magazine and then looked quite angrily

at Valdini. 'Do you realise this thing is loaded?' He shook his head, muttered something about 'Damn fool thing to do,' and handed the gun and the magazine separately back to Valdini.

His complete unawareness of anything serious behind the gun in Valdini's hand acted like a douche of cold water. The tension eased. Mayne picked up his drink again. Carla relaxed. We all began to move and talk naturally again. It was as though a group of puppets had suddenly come to life. The room itself seemed to sigh with relief. 'Just in time, Joe,' Engles said. 'Valdini was showing us how a Sicilian gangster draws a gun. What are you having?' he added, ignoring the black look Valdini gave him.

'I'll have a cognac,' Joe grunted. He had a puzzled frown on his face. 'Why ever did you let that little bastard play around with that gun?' he whispered as he pushed his way between Engles and myself. 'I suppose everybody carries a gun in this damned country. But they ought to know better than to fool around with them.'

He handed Engles two rolls of films. 'A few shots I did of the *slittovia* and also some interior shots of this room. Take a look at them. They're not bad.' A third roll he passed across to me. 'Want to see yourself in a state of collapse? It wants more light. But it's a good action shot. It grips, even though you do play it down a bit.' He drank his cognac. When he had set his glass down he said, 'Well, may as well go and develop some of the other rolls. Can't do anything else in this weather. Wish I'd a camera with me when I came in just now. I'd like to have got a shot of little Valdini with that gun. Somehow, it all looked so real. Might let me know what you think of those shots, old man.'

'I will,' Engles said. And Joe heaved himself out of the room.

I glanced round the room. It all looked quite peaceful now. Mayne had gone over to the piano and was quietly drifting through a piece I did not recognise. Carla was talking excitedly to Valdini. Keramikos was sipping an anisette at the other end of the bar. A chord crashed out from the piano and Mayne switched with a malicious sense of humour into *La Donna Immobile*. 'The pot is boiling all right,' Engles said quietly. 'One more scene like that and there really will be some shooting. Valdini is not the only one who has a gun, I'm pretty certain about that.'

'What's all this about a million in gold?' I asked. Our conversation was masked by the sound of the piano.

'Remember those cuttings from the *Corriere della Venezia* you sent me? One of them has a reference to it. It was the consignment from the bank at Venice. Part of it disappeared *en route*. The actual spot where it disappeared was the Tre Croci Pass. This bunch of carrion are here because of it. Mayne, Keramikos, the Contessa and Valdini—they all know about it. They all think it's somewhere up here. The interesting point is—who actually knows where it is?'

'Do you know?' I asked.

He shook his head. 'No. As far as I am concerned, it was just a hunch, based on the news that Stelben owned Col da Varda. You see, when Stelben was originally arrested, I interrogated him in Milan. It was this story of the missing gold that interested us. I spent a lot of time on the case. I even went to Berlin and saw—' At that moment Mayne stopped playing. There was a sudden silence. The howl of the wind outside invaded the room. It was a dismal, nerve-racking sound. Beyond the windows, the snowflakes sped by in a never-ending stream. 'Better go on playing,' Engles said to Mayne, 'or everybody will start screaming at each other again.'

Mayne nodded quite cheerfully. He seemed perfectly at ease again. He settled himself on the stool and plunged into *Symphonie Fantastique*. Keramikos sidled along the bar. 'Will you please tell me, Mr Engles, what was the cause of the trouble between the Contessa Forelli and Mayne?' he asked.

Engles gave him a quick resumé of what had occurred. When he had finished, Keramikos nodded. 'Ah! It is the thought of all that gold that made her mad. She will have been called worse things than a prostitute in her life. So she does not know where

113

it is, eh?' He thrust his head forward suddenly. 'Do you know where it is, Mr Engles?'

'If I did, you would hardly expect me to tell you,' Engles replied.

Keramikos gave a short laugh that was more like a grunt. 'Of course not, my friend. But we should help each other a little, you and I. These people here—'and he nodded in the direction of the Contessa and Mayne—'they are only interested for themselves. With them it is self-interest. Whereas you and I, we have a mission. We do not work for ourselves.'

'And who are you working for now, Keramikos?' Engles asked.

'For my country,' he replied. 'Always for my country.' He peered more closely at Engles. 'You remember that we have met before, eh?'

'Of course I do,' Engles replied. 'It was at the Piraeus. You had some ELAS guerillas with you and were attempting to mine the harbour at night.'

'Ah—I thought you had not forgotten. It was cold that night. The harbour water was black and full of oil and dirt. It tasted very unpleasant. I did not enjoy that swim.' He smiled. 'And now we drink together. Do you not find that strange?'

'It's not always possible to choose one's drinking company,' Engles replied blandly.

Keramikos gave a fat chuckle and his little eyes twinkled behind the thick lenses. 'That is life,' he said. 'You serve your Government. I serve mine. Our meetings should be dramatic moments—with pistols, like Valdini. Instead, we drink.'

'Don't be absurd, Keramikos,' Engles said. 'You have no Government left to serve.'

Keramikos sighed. 'That is true. That is very true. For the moment there is nothing left—just a loose organisation under the ground. But there are many Germans working, like myself, all over the world. We work without direction and without funds. That will change in time. At the moment our energy is wasted in the search for money. That is why I am here. I have an organisation in Greece. It must be paid, if it is to continue. Four million dollars in gold would help. But it will not always be like this. Some day Germany will begin to organise again. And next time—the third time—perhaps we shall not fail. Already you are saying that Germany must be prosperous so that she can take her place in the economic plan of Europe. We have no national debt like you. Each war has been paid for in the ruins of defeat. We starve now, and that means that the old people die. And that again is good for a nation. Our industry is destroyed. That, too, is good. Our, industry, when we rebuild it, will be new and up-to-date, not old works adjusted to meet the changing needs, like yours. It will be the same with our armed forces. You will see. Last time it was twenty years. Twenty years is a long time. There will be a new generation then who will not remember that war is horrible.'

'You're very frank about it,' Engles said.

'And why not? You are a Colonel in the British Intelligence.'

'Was,' Engles corrected him. 'I'm a civilian now.'

Keramikos shrugged his shoulders. 'What does it matter what you call yourself? I call myself a shipping agent. But you remain of the Intelligence, and you must know that your people are aware that we exist. But what can they do? For example, what can they do about me? I am a Greek national. Greece is a free country. They cannot arrest me. And I shall do nothing foolish here in Italy. I shall get the gold. But I shall be careful. I shall not kill any one—if it can be avoided. Mayne and Valdini are different. They are both gangsters, and dangerous. Mayne is a deserter, as I told Blair.'

'Yes, I know all about Mayne,' Engles said. 'What I am interested in is how you found out about this gold. You couldn't have learned about it in Greece.'

'I could not, eh?' He seemed amused. 'Yet this is the first time I have been out of Greece since I went to Alexandria. And that was a long time ago—just before the Greek mutiny. No, I heard about it in Greece. It was luck. The one man who escaped out of the wretched guard that brought the gold up from Venice sought the help of my people in Salonika. They asked him to account for himself. And he broke down under questioning. But you know the story of how Stelben got that gold, eh?'

'Only by deduction,' Engles replied. 'Not from evidence. Stelben kept his mouth shut. And I certainly didn't know any of the guard escaped. He even murdered his personal servant who had been with him for nearly six years. I'd like to know what your man had to tell. And Blair here knows nothing of the story as yet.'

'Ah! Then you shall read the statement of the Korporal who escaped. And we will have a drink to fortify ourselves, eh?' He ordered the drinks and I leaned closer, for Mayne had gone into something loud and sonorous, which, with the noise of the wind outside, made it difficult to hear.

When Aldo had put the drinks in front of us, Keramikos said, 'This does not reflect well on the *Gestapo*. But all organisations, you understand, have their bad servants. You must remember it was near the end. And Stelben had killed many people before he shot down those nine soldiers. The gold was at a bank in Venice. It was the property of one of the Rome banking houses and had been transported to Venice for greater safety after your troops landed at Anzio. When we fell back to the line of the Po River, Heinrich Stelben was instructed to convey the gold to the Reichsbank at Munich. He was to take it by road, for you were bombarding the railways from the air, and the route chosen was through Cortina and Bolzano to Innsbruck. You must picture to yourselves that little convoy. There was the truck containing the gold. It was closed and sealed. And two *volkswagen*. And there were seven honest German *soldaten* and Stelben—and gold to the value of over eight million dollars.'

7

The Story of the Gold

Keramikos paused and glanced quickly round. Mayne was playing *Danse Macabre* now. The Contessa and Valdini were still talking together. And the snow streamed past the windows and piled up in great drifts on the belvedere. Then he took an old leather wallet from his pocket and brought out a folded sheet of foolscap. He smoothed it out on the bar and handed it to Engles. 'That is the statement made by Korporal Holtz of the Panzer Grenadiers,' he said. 'You may read it.'

Engles placed it on the bar so that I could read it over his shoulder. It was typewritten and in German. It was dated 9th October, 1945. I reproduce it here because I happen to have it with me as I write and because it is a good statement. Holtz tells the story with a directness and simplicity of wording often to be found in statements from soldiers. And this, combined with the noise of the wind and Mayne playing, made the scene he described very vivid to me as I read it, there in that bar-room, right over the spot where it had happened. It was, as Keramikos said, not a pretty story and it invested the old with a peculiarly live quality that must, I think, be possessed by all things which have inspired greed and caused the death of many people.

Statement concerning the events which took place on the night of 15-16th March, 1945, at the Passo Tre Croci made by Korporal Holtz, H. V. of the 9th Panzer Grenadiers.

(Translation of the German original taken from the body of Keramikos, the Greek.)

117

On 15th March, 1945, I was ordered to report with a guard of three men to Kapitan Heinrich Stelben at the Albergo Daniele, Venice. Kapitan Stelben ordered me to proceed to the Banca Commerciale del Popolo and take charge of forty wooden cases containing gold. As soon as it was dark, we loaded the cases on to a launch and proceeded to the Piazzale Roma. Here we transferred the boxes to a closed truck, which was then sealed by Kapitan Stelben and an official of the bank in my presence. The Kapitan then gave me the route, which was by Mestre-Conigliamo-Cortina-Bolzano-Innsbruck to Munich. Besides the sealed truck there were two *volkswagen*. One of these, with a driver, was assigned to me and I was instructed to lead. Next came the truck containing the gold with a driver and one of my men as guard. In the rear was Kapitan Stelben in the other *volkswagen* with a driver and my other two men. The drivers were all German. I do not know their names. The names of my men were Soldaten Flick, Wrenner and Reinbaum.

At Ponte nelle Alpi we stopped to put on chains. The roads had a thick coating of snow as we climbed into the mountains. It was freezing and the surface was slippery. Shortly after Cortina, Kapitan Stelben ordered us to halt by blowing on his horn. It was just after two o'clock in the morning. We were at the top of a pass. I examined my map and identified it as the Tre Croci Pass and the big square block of buildings we had just passed as the Tre Croci Hotel.

The Kapitan drove up alongside my car and informed me that he had been given sealed instructions to be opened at this spot. He produced an envelope and opened it. He then informed me that he was ordered to place the gold under guard in a concrete building at the top of a cable sleigh nearby. He then took the lead and we branched off the main road on to a track. Within a few hundred metres we reached a concrete building and were challenged by a sentry.

The Kapitan explained his instructions and the sentry called the Korporal of the guard. When the Korporal came out, Kapitan Stelben handed him the instructions. The Korporal appeared puzzled and stated that he must speak with his officer, who was billeted at the hotel. The Kapitan informed him that such a delay was impossible and referred him to the instructions, which apparently stated that the gold must be transferred with the least possible delay and its storage completed before first light. He said that as soon as the gold had been stored he himself would accompany the Korporal of the guard to interview his officer.

To this the Korporal agreed. We then broke the seals of the truck and proceeded to off-load the cases of gold and transfer them to the sleigh, the whole of the guard, which consisted of only two men and the Korporal, assisting. Whilst this was in progress, the Korporal approached me and expressed concern that he had not been permitted to report to his officer. He was a Bavarian and belonged to an anti-aircraft unit which had taken over from the ski troops who had been training there. They were building heavy flak positions at the top of the *slittovia*. He pointed out to me that it was strange that he had not been warned to expect the arrival of such an important convoy and, after some discussion, I became uneasy in my mind, especially as my men were openly grumbling because they had been led to believe that they were proceeding to Germany.

The sleigh would only take half the gold. And when this was loaded, I went with the Korporal of the guard to the Kapitan. The Korporal insisted that he be permitted to report to his officer. Kapitan Stelben at first refused permission. He became very angry and threatened the Korporal with punishment for obstructing the work of the *Gestapo*. I pointed out to the Kapitan that the absence of the Korporal would not interrupt the transfer of the gold, especially as one of the men of the guard was capable of driving the sleigh.

In the end Kapitan Stelben agreed to accompany the Korporal forthwith to see his officer. He instructed me to proceed to the top with the first load. I was to leave one of my men with the remaining guard in charge of the trucks. He then departed with the Korporal.

I posted my man on the truck containing the gold and, with the rest, boarded the sleigh. At the top of the *slittovia* was a building, like a concrete emplacement, which housed the haulage machinery. Near it was a small refuge hut, and just above this were earth workings where the flak guns were being installed. We had barely completed the unloading when the telephone rang in the machine-room. I went in and answered it. It was the Kapitan. He ordered me to have the boxes moved to the edge of the deepest of the pits dug for the concrete gun platforms. Whilst my men were doing this, I was to send the sleigh back for him. This I did and ordered the men to move the boxes to the gun positions. A path had been worn from the top of the *slittovia* to these workings. But it was very slippery. The slope was steep and the boxes difficult to manage. My men grumbled a great deal.

We had not completed this work when the Kapitan arrived. He complained that we were slow. And he kept glancing at his watch. He seemed agitated. The men grumbled even in front of him and he blamed me for not having control.

When the work was completed and the boxes stacked round the pit, he said, 'Parade your men in the machine-room, Korporal. I want a word with them.' I did this, parading them in a single line on the far side of the room where there was a little space. I was nervous and so were the men. Discipline was not good at this stage of the war, but we were still afraid of the *Gestapo*. The Kapitan gave an order to the driver of the sleigh and he came in with a sheepish look.

Then the Kapitan entered and shut the door. His face twitched and I noticed that there was blood on his tunic and on his left hand. I thought he had fallen and cut himself. He seemed irritable and plucked nervously at the sling of the automatic gun on his shoulder. 'One of the cases in the truck has been opened and some gold is missing,' he said. 'I am going to search each of you in turn. About turn!' We turned automatically so that we were facing the blank concrete wall.

For some reason I turned my head. I saw then that he had the gun in his hands. At the same moment that I turned, he began firing. I sprang at the naked electric light bulb which was fixed to a wall socket just above my head. I hit it with my fist. In doing this I tripped over a piece of machinery and fell against the cable drum. The room was completely dark. It was full of smoke and the noise of the gun was very loud in that confined space. I felt half stunned, for I had hit my head.

A torch was switched on. I lay still. I could see the Kapitan through a gap in a large wheel against which I was lying. He climbed over to the wall and began examining the bodies, one by one. He had his torch in one hand and his revolver in the other. The door was quite near me. I slid quietly along the floor behind the cable drum and reached it. He turned and fired as I opened it. The bullet hit me in the arm. I staggered out and then felt myself falling. I rolled over and over down a steep slope and finished up in soft snow. I had fallen down the sleigh track.

I climbed into the shelter of the woods. Shortly afterwards the sleigh came down. Kapitan Stelben was driving it, and two bodies lay across one of the seats. A few minutes later firing broke out at the bottom of the *slittovia*. When everything was quiet, I went out on to the sleigh track. But someone was coming up, pulling himself up by the cable. He passed quite close to me and I saw that it was the Kapitan again.

I then made my way down through the woods. At the bottom I found the Korporal, who had gone with the Kapitan to see his officer, lying on his face. The snow was red under his head. He had a bayonet wound in the throat. A little farther on there were more bodies. One had been garrotted. The other two had been killed by bullets. One was the Kapitan's personal servant and the other the man who had driven the sleigh.

I was very frightened at the sight of these dead bodies and at the memory of what had happened at the top of the *slittovia*. I was afraid my story would not be believed. I bound up my wound, which I discovered to be only slight, and had the good fortune to obtain a lift in a truck going down into Italy. This took me to Trieste and from there I managed to obtain passage in a *caique* bound for Corfu. Later, in civilian clothes, I took passage in a schooner for Salonika, where I had been stationed in 1941 and knew people who might help me.

I hereby swear that the above is a true record of what occurred. This is the first statement I have ever made concerning the events described and at no time have I ever mentioned the matter to any one in whole or in part.

Signed: HANS HOLTZ.

At Salonika,
9 – 10 – 45.

When we had finished reading the statement, Engles carefully folded the sheet of paper and handed it back to Keramikos. 'It's strange to see it all written down,' he said. 'I was convinced that that was roughly what had happened. But I couldn't prove it. Stelben's statement was that, shortly after passing the Tre Croci Hotel, they were forced to a stop because a lorry was drawn up across the road. His men mutinied and joined the men from the lorry. He and his servant, joined by the guard from the *slittovia*, attempted to prevent them getting at the gold. There was a fight. The *slittovia* guard and his servant were killed. He was bound and taken up to the top of the *slittovia*. He managed to free himself eventually and at seven-thirty in the morning he staggered into the Tre Croci Hotel. That was the statement he made to the Commandant of the anti-aircraft unit at Tre Croci. Later he went on with the remaining nineteen cases of gold to Innsbruck, where he made a similar statement to the *Gestapo*.'

'Yes, I heard about the statement,' Keramikos said. 'One of my people had seen it. Did the *Gestapo* arrest him?'

'No. Things were a bit chaotic at the time and he was urgently required in Italy to deal with the threatened Communist risings in the big towns. I interrogated him, you know, when he was first arrested. I could never shake him from that statement. Its weakness was, of course, that they would never have troubled to take him up to the top of the *slittovia*.' Engles looked at Keramikos with a puzzled frown. 'Just why did you show me Holtz's statement?' he asked.

'Ah—you are thinking that it tells you where the gold is hidden, eh?'

'By the time he had killed those men up here and taken the bodies down to the bottom and then climbed all the way back, it could not have been earlier than, say, four o'clock. He reported to the Commandant at the Tre Croci Hotel at seven-thirty. That gives him barely three hours in which to bury the five remaining bodies and twenty-one cases of gold. He wouldn't have had time to move those boxes to another hiding place.'

Keramikos shrugged his shoulders. 'Perhaps you are right,' he said.

'Then why did you show me the statement?'

'Because, my friend, it only tells you where the gold was. It does not tell you where it is now. Don't forget that Stelben owned this place for a short time. And he had two Germans working for him up here. They were here for over two weeks before they were arrested.'

'Were they alone here?'

'Yes. Aldo and his wife and Anna were given a month's holiday.'

'Strange that the two Germans should have been killed in that riot at the Regina Coeli.'

Keramikos smiled. 'Yes,' he said. 'Very convenient, eh—for someone. But who?'

At that moment Carla interrupted us. 'You have secrets that you talk together so quietly—yes?'

'No secrets from you, Carla,' Engles replied. 'We were just wondering what your little Heinrich did with the bodies of the five German soldiers he buried up here.'

'What do you mean?'

'Don't pretend that you know nothing about it. Where did he put them—and the gold?'

'How should I know?' She was tense and her fingers were tearing at a button on her scarlet suit.

'Weren't you here when he had those two Germans working for him?' Engles asked.

'No. I was in Venice.'

'He did not trust you, eh?' Keramikos said with a sly smile. She made no answer.

Engles turned to Valdini, who had moved quietly over to join us. 'And where were you?' he asked.

'I also was in Venice,' Valdini replied. He was watching Carla and there was an ugly little grin on his face.

'You were in Cortina.' Carla's voice sounded startled.

'No,' he said, still with that evil grin. 'I was in Venice.'

'But I told you to go to Cortina. You said you were at Cortina.' She was very agitated.

'I was in Venice,' he repeated, and his eyes watched her coldly, like a snake.

'Ah,' said Keramikos. 'You were told to keep an eye on Stelben and his two friends. Yet you remained in Venice. I wonder why.'

'There was no need to go to Cortina. The two Germans were friends of Mayne's. They were looking after her interests—and Mayne's.'

I heard Mayne miss a note, and I glanced towards the piano. He was watching us and, as I looked at him, he stopped playing and got up. The others had not noticed. They were watching Valdini. And the little Sicilian was watching Carla.

'So you stayed in Venice?' Keramikos said. 'Why in Venice?'

'I wished to keep an eye on Mayne,' Valdini replied slowly.

'You were spying on me,' Carla snarled in Italian. 'Why were you spying on me?'

The corners of his eyes crinkled and his neat little figure was swelled out. He was enjoying himself. 'You think you can make the fool of me,' he said to her in English. His tone was violent. 'You think I have no pride. Once you were glad to say, *Si, si, Signor Valdini*. That was when I owned you and fifty gairls like you. And when I permitted you to call me Stefan—how you were overcome with delight! I did not mind Stelben and all those others. That was business. But this is different. I do not trust you now.'

'You say Mayne was in Venice,' Engles said. 'What was he doing there?'

'Making love to Carla,' Valdini replied, and his lips were drawn back from his discoloured teeth in an expression of disgust.

Carla hit him then. She hit him with the back of her hand, and the big diamond ring blazed a trail of blood across his cheek.

But he caught her wrist and, with a quick stoop of his body, threw her over his shoulder. Her head hit the bar rail with a sickening thud. He rushed over to where she lay groaning and began to hack at her ribs with the pointed toe of his shoe. 'You leave me for a dirty little English deserter who does not care for anything but the gold,' he screamed at her in Italian. He was beside himself with rage, literally crying with anger. 'Why didn't you trust me? I would have found it for you. But now—'

Before any of us had begun to move, Mayne had crossed the room. He caught Valdini by the collar of his jacket, swung him round and hit him with his fist between the eyes. The Sicilian was flung back against the wall, where he slowly subsided like a sack. Mayne turned and faced us. His eyes were watchful and he had his right hand in the pocket of his jacket.

'Be careful now,' Engles whispered in my ear. 'The pot has boiled over and he's got a gun.' His voice was excited. He turned to Mayne. 'Those two Germans,' he said. 'Would their names be—Wilhelm Muller and Friedrich Mann?' He shot the names out like a prosecuting counsel making his final point in a murder trial.

And the effect on Mayne was noticeable. His face looked pinched and grey in that cold light and he kept nervous watch on the whole room.

'You put Carla in touch with those two,' Engles continued. His voice was cold and matter-of-fact. 'She introduced them to Stelben. And Stelben was glad to use them because they were gangsters and there would be no questions when they disappeared. He did not know they were your men. When they had found out what you wanted to know, you had them arrested with Stelben.'

'And I suppose I arranged for them to be shot in that prison riot?' he sneered.

'You were in Rome at the time,' Carla suddenly said. She had struggled on to one elbow and was watching him malevolently.

'It could have been arranged,' Engles said, 'if you had known the right people. And I think you did know the right people.'

'And why do you think that?' Mayne was watching only Engles now. He was not sure of himself. I wished Engles would leave it at that. The situation was getting ugly.

'Because,' Engles said slowly, 'you are not Gilbert Mayne.'

'And who am I, then?' Mayne's left hand was clenched.

'You're a murderer and a gangster,' Engles snapped back. 'We nearly caught you in Naples in 1944. You had deserted during the Salerno landing and were running a gang in the dock area of Naples. You were wanted for murder and robbery. You were also wanted for smuggling German prisoners through the lines. That was why I became interested in your activities. We got you in Rome three months after the city fell. You and your girl were picked up in a *trattoria*. That's where you got that bullet scar. I interrogated you. You recognised me when I arrived here, but you thought I might not recognise you because your head was bandaged when I last saw you.'

'This is ridiculous,' Mayne said. He was struggling to regain his habitual ease of manner. 'You are mistaking me for someone else. My military career was quite straightforward. I was a captain in the Artillery. I was taken prisoner and after my escape I joined UNRRA. You can check the War Office records.'

'I did that before I left England,' Engles said quietly. 'Captain Gilbert Mayne was reported missing in January, 1944. He was believed killed in action near Cassino. Two months later he is recorded as having escaped from a German prison camp. You pretended to be suffering from shock when you reported for duty as Captain Mayne, and were allowed to join UNRRA. You applied to be sent to Greece, where there was little likelihood of your meeting up with any of the officers of Gilbert Mayne's ack-ack regiment. I suggest that Gilbert Mayne was, in fact, killed in action. Your name is Stuart Ross—and Muller and Mann were members of your Naples gang.'

Mayne laughed. It was a wild laugh. He was white and very tense. 'First you accuse me of trying to murder Blair and planning to murder Carla. Now you—'

'It is true,' Carla interrupted him hoarsely. 'Everything he has said is true. I know it is true.' She had struggled to her feet. Her face was grey under her make-up and she was very close to tears. 'You wished to keel me. You said you would find out where the gold was. You said you loved me. You said we would discover the gold and then we would marry and share it. But you lied.' Her voice trembled on the edge of hysteria. 'All the time you lie to me. It was you who bought Col da Varda at the auction. I discovered that yesterday. And—it is you who know where the gold is. You—you,' she screamed. 'May it do you the good it has done the others.'

Mayne went across to her. There was no doubt of his intentions. He was livid with anger. He raised his hand to hit her. And as he took it out of his pocket, Valdini, who had recovered consciousness, went for his gun. It was in an armpit holster and because he was still dazed he fumbled the draw. Mayne was

127

quicker. He shot him before he had even got his gun out of its holster. He shot him in the chest. A little black mark appeared suddenly on the brilliant blue of Valdini's jacket, and he gave a grunt and rolled over.

Nobody moved for a moment. The smoke curled up blue from Mayne's gun. The shattering sound of the shot seemed to have immobilised us all. Valdini began to whimper and cough up blood.

Carla was the first to move. She gave a little cry and knelt down beside Valdini. We watched her lift his head and wipe the blood from his mouth with the yellow silk handkerchief from his breast pocket. He opened his eyes and looked up at her. '*Carla—cara mia.*' He tried to smile at her and then his head fell back, loose and relaxed.

'Stefan!' she cried out. 'Stefan! Don't leave me.'

But he was dead.

She looked up then, still holding his body in her arms. And she was crying. I think that was the most shocking part of the whole business—that she should be crying because Stefan Valdini was dead.

'Why did you have to kill him?' Her voice sounded tired. 'He loved me. My poor Stefan! He was all I had really. All I've ever had. He was mine. He was the only one who really loved me. He was like a puppy. Why did you have to kill him?'

She seemed to take a grip on herself then. She laid Valdini's body back on the floor and got to her feet. Then she went slowly towards Mayne. He was watching her and at the same time trying to watch us, the gun still in his hand. When she was close to him, she stopped. Her eyes were big and wild-looking. 'You fool!' she said. 'We might have killed Heinrich quietly and shared all that gold between the two of us. We might have been very happy for all of our lives. Why did you have to have Heinrich arrested? And those two friends of yours? It was all so public.'

'The sight of that gold was too much for my two friends,' Mayne replied harshly.

Carla sighed. 'All my life I have lived with men who cheated and killed. But I thought you were honest. I thought you really loved me. In Venice—I was so happy at the thought that we should be rich and be able to live well and without danger. Then you went away and Heinrich and your two friends were arrested. I became suspicious then. I had Stefan follow you. Then I knew that it was all over, that it was not me you loved—only the gold. You bid against me for this place. You planned to murder Stefan and myself. You are a dirty lying cheat.' She said these words without emotion. But her voice rose as she went on, 'Now you have killed Stefan. Why don't you kill me too? You have a gun. You should not be afraid with a gun in your hand. Go on, kill me, why don't you?' She laughed. 'You fool, Gilbert! You should kill me now—and all these others. Think of all that gold—and then remember that you are the only person left who knows where it is.' She smiled bitterly. 'It will do you no good. *Arrivederci*, Gilbert.'

She turned and walked slowly out of the room.

We watched her go. I don't know about the others, but my nails bit deep into the palms of my hands as I waited, tensed, for Mayne to fire. His face was white and sullen and I could feel the pressure of his finger on the trigger of that pistol as he slowly lifted it. Then suddenly he relaxed and let the gun fall to his side. Carla's ski boots sounded on the bare boards of the passage outside and then climbed slowly up the stairs.

He turned to us with a smile. It was meant to be an easy, confident smile. But all he achieved was a deathly grin. His face looked drawn and hollow. His skin had a grey pallor that was not entirely due to the dim, snow-whitened light that came through the windows from the bleak world outside. And I suddenly realised that he was afraid.

He seemed to hesitate for a moment. I think he was debating whether to shoot us down there and then. I had an unpleasant sensation in the pit of my stomach. 'If he raises that gun, dive for the table,' Engles whispered to me. His voice was tense. I glanced at the big pine table. It offered very little cover. I felt helpless and I think I was frightened. My mouth felt dry and every movement, every sound in that room was magnified so that the scene is still quite vivid in my mind.

I remember I could hear the ticking of the cuckoo clock above the noise of the wind. I believe the sound of the snow falling was actually audible, a dull blanketed murmur that was like a sigh. And there was a strange chattering noise, which I traced to Aldo's teeth. The blood was moving in a dark trickle from below Valdini's mouth, which was open and resting close against the scrubbed pine boards of the floor. One of us had spilled a glass of cognac on the bar. The little pool of liquor dripped steadily on to the floor.

It seemed ages that we stood there like that—quite still—the three of us bunched against the bar, Aldo with a cloth in one hand and a glass in the other and his teeth chattering in his bald shiny head, and Mayne standing out there in the middle of the room, the gun slack in his hand. But I suppose it was only for a matter of seconds really. A door shut and Carla's boots sounded overhead. She was in Valdini's room.

Mayne glanced up. He, too, was listening to the sound of those footsteps, and I think he must have been wishing that he had killed her whilst he had the chance. Then he pulled himself together. And it was with something of his old manner that he turned to us and said, 'I am afraid, gentlemen, I shall have to ask you to hand over your weapons, if any. You first, Keramikos! Step over to the table where I can see you clearly.' And he motioned him to move with the point of his gun. 'You needn't be afraid,' he added as the Greek hesitated. 'I won't shoot you. I'll need your help in digging up the gold.'

I think Keramikos was in two minds. By a quick movement he could get behind Engles. But Engles had turned and was watching him.

'You'd better do it before he gets frightened again,' Engles said.

Keramikos suddenly smiled. 'Yes, perhaps it is better,' he said and went over to the table. He glanced enquiringly at Mayne.

'Take your gun out by the muzzle and lay it on the table,' Mayne told him.

Keramikos did this.

'Now turn round.'

I half braced myself for the shot. But Mayne walked over to him and searched him quickly with practised hands.

It was Engles' turn next. He, too, had a gun.

'Now you, Blair.'

'I haven't got a gun,' I said as I went over to the table.

He laughed at that. 'Bit of a sheep among the wolves, aren't you?' he said. But he searched me all the same. He even ordered Aldo out from behind the bar and searched him. The Italian was practically beside himself with fear, and, as he came out from behind the bar, his eyes were starting in his head so that he looked like some grotesque doll out of a Russian ballet. 'Now get that body out of here,' Mayne told Aldo in Italian. 'Bury it in the snow and wash those boards.'

'*Non, non, signore. Mamma mia! E non possibile.*' I don't know which he was more terrified of—Mayne's gun or the body huddled against the wall in its pool of blood. He was gibbering and quite beyond reason.

Mayne turned to us. 'There's no sense in this animal,' he said. 'Perhaps you'd be good enough to dump it outside in the snow somewhere so that it doesn't show and get this *cretino* to swab the floor.' He was quite master of himself again. He dealt with the disposal of Valdini's body as though it were a glass that had been smashed. 'Do not try to go to your rooms yet,' he added. 'I want to search them first.' He glanced up. Carla's boots were moving about almost directly above his head. 'Now I must go up and attend to Carla,' he said. But first he went to the telephone and wrenched it out of the wall.

'What are you going to do to her?' Engles asked as he made for the door.

He turned in the doorway and smiled. 'Make love to her,' he said. And we heard his boots on the boards outside and then on the stairs. There was the crash of a door being kicked open and then a scream that was instantly stifled. It became a moaning sound that was gradually lost in the noise of the wind.

'*Mein Gott*! He has killed her,' Keramikos said.

We stood, listening. Whatever a woman may be, it is not pleasant to hear her scream with pain and to think that she has been killed without any attempt being made to prevent it. I felt suddenly very sick. That scream and Valdini's body lying there like a stuck pig in his own blood—it was too much. Footsteps sounded on the stairs again. Mayne was coming back. He entered the room and stopped as he saw that none of us had moved. 'What's the matter with you people?' he asked. He had put his gun away and seemed almost cheerful.

'Have you killed her?' Engles asked.

'Good God, no! Just tied her up, that's all. She couldn't find another gun in Valdini's room.' He nodded at the body. 'Engles! Will you and Blair remove that. Keramikos—you come with me.'

Valdini's body was not heavy. We opened the window by the bar and pitched it out. There was a deep drift and Valdini sank into it as though it were a feather bed. I leaned out of the window and looked down at him. He was sprawled on his back, his clothes very bright against the white background of the snow and the blood from his mouth making a red stain round his head. He looked like a rag doll with a ridiculous scarlet hat set at a jaunty angle on its head. Then the snow began to drift across him and his body became indistinct. The wind was very cold on my face and rapidly crusted my head with driven snow. I stepped back and closed the window. Engles was standing over Aldo. The Italian was on his knees, swabbing up the blood with a bar cloth. 'I think I need a drink,' I said.

'Pour me one, will you?' He came over to the bar. 'Must be near lunch time.'

I glanced at the cuckoo clock, which was still ticking away merrily as though nothing had happened. It was twelve-thirty. 'I have never felt less like food,' I said.

'Good God! You've seen worse than this,' he said as he took the drink I handed him.

'I know,' I said. 'But that was war. I suppose one gets used to the idea of death during one's battle training. But killing a man in cold blood, that's different. I thought he was going to shoot her.'

'Don't worry—he will. And he'll shoot us, too, if we don't do something about it.' He raised his glass. 'Cheers!' he said. He was quite cool. 'It's a funny thing,' he said, 'the effect that gold or jewels, or any form of concentrated wealth, has on men. Take our friend Stelben; he slaughtered nine men, as casually as you or I would cut a film script. It's the same with Mayne. Already he's killed three men and caused another to commit suicide. That's the straightforward killer for you—the gangster, the man who kills without thought or feeling. He's a pretty dull fellow really, no emotions. It's only what he does that's exciting.'

'Why the devil did you want to get involved in this business?' I said.

He gave me a quick glance. 'Yes, I was afraid you'd ask that sooner or later.' He hesitated. 'You know, I've been wondering about it myself during the past few minutes. Pride, I suppose, and my insatiable desire for excitement. I had a good record as an Intelligence officer, you know. I didn't fall down on many things. But I did fall down on the matter of Stelben and his gold. And when I read of his arrest and how he had become the owner of Col da Varda, something told me the scent was hot again. I just had to do something about it. And then, when you sent me that photograph, I knew I was right. I recognised Mayne and I thought I recognised Keramikos. I just had to come over and see what was going on. But when I talked this morning about stoking up the fires, it never occurred to me that things would move so swiftly.' He patted me on the shoulder. 'Sorry!'

he added. 'I didn't mean to land you in a mess like this. Make no mistake about it, Neil—we're in a pretty tight spot.'

'Well, let's get out of it,' I said.

'How?'

'Surely we could make Tre Croci on skis?'

'Yes, on skis. But Mayne is no fool. He will have thought of that, and of the snow-shoes. However, let's investigate.'

He was quite right. Mayne was standing by the open door of the ski room and the clatter of skis told us that he had Keramikos at work tying them up. 'Disposed of the body?' he asked. 'Then come and give a hand with these.' He kept well clear of us as we entered the little room and his eyes were watchful. There were several pairs of skis there besides our own. We tied them in bundles of three and then he had us carry them out on to the belvedere.

Mayne directed us to the concrete machine-room at the top of the *slittovia*. The snow was very deep, in places over our knees. He unlocked the door for us and we filed in, glad to get out of that biting, snow-laden wind. The place felt chill and damp, and it had that musty smell that all unused concrete buildings have. The machinery was covered with a grey film of concrete dust so that it looked old and disused. But it was well oiled. The snow clung like a white veil to the windows, which were heavily barred. The wind whistled through the slit by which the cable entered. I glanced at the opposite wall. That was where Stelben had shot down those German soldiers, according to the statement of Korporal Holtz. But there were no bullet marks. The concrete presented a smooth, grey, uninteresting front. Engles must have noticed my interest, for he whispered, 'Looks as though Stelben had that re-cemented.'

We stacked the skis and the two pairs of snow-shoes in the corner by the switchboard. Then we went out into the snow again and Mayne locked the door. We fought our way back in the teeth of the wind to the belvedere. Mayne paused at the entrance to the hut. 'We'll start work this afternoon,' he said. 'In the meantime, I'd be glad if you'd stick around the bar as far as possible, so that I can keep an eye on you.'

We went in then. The big room seemed warm. We shook the snow off our clothes and it melted in pools on the floor. Joe was at the bar. 'Where the hell have you all been?' he asked us. 'And what's the matter with Aldo? He's even more stupid than usual. He's broken two glasses and fumbled a bottle of cognac.' Anna was laying the table. She gave us a scared look. The colour had drained out of her face and it no longer looked bright and cheerful. Joe ordered drinks and produced several rolls of film. 'Some ski-ing shots,' he grunted as we moved over to the bar. 'Gives you some idea of the possibilities of the place.' He handed them to Engles.

'Where have you been doing your developing?' Engles asked.

'Out at the back, in the scullery,' he said. 'Cold as charity. But it's got running water.'

Apparently he had heard nothing. Engles began running through the negatives. Mayne stood apart from us. It was strange, standing there drinking with someone who had heard nothing and was completely unaware that anything out of the ordinary had happened.

Engles suddenly stopped half-way through the second roll of film. 'What's this shot, Joe?' he asked.

Joe leaned over and glanced at the celluloid. 'Oh, that's a picture I took the night we arrived. Good moonlight shot. Went out and took it from the trees at the edge of the *slittovia*. Good spooky stuff, isn't it?'

'Ye-es—it is.' Engles was peering at it closely. 'What's he doing?' He pointed to one of the negatives with his finger.

Joe looked at it over his shoulder. 'Dunno,' he said.

'Seemed to be measuring something. Gives a bit of action to it. Matter of fact, that was why I went out. Wanted to get some-body moving around the place to give it a little life.'

'Did he know you were taking pictures?'

135

'Good Lord, no! Would have spoilt it. He wouldn't have moved naturally.'

'Good point.' Engles passed the film across to me. 'Nice shot there, Neil. Might give you an idea or two. Ought to have a moonlight episode in the script. Film very effectively.'

I took the length of film from his hands. His thumb was placed on one of the shots to indicate a figure bending down. I held the celluloid up to the light. It showed the whole front of the *rifugio* with its high snow-crusted gables, the great pine supports and, in the centre, the concrete housing of the *slittovia* machinery over which the hut had been built. The moonlight reflected white in the windows of the machine-room, and outlined against them was the figure of a man. It was not difficult to recognise that small, neat figure. It was Valdini.

I ran quickly down the strip of celluloid. He had his arms stretched out and made the motions of a man measuring the outside of the concrete housing. I could even see what appeared to be a measuring tape in his hands. Then he got to his feet and went round to the side of the building. The outside edge of the door suddenly appeared in the film and Valdini disappeared.

'Not bad, eh?' Engles said. 'Might run through the rest of it. There are one or two good ski-ing shots on that one.' He was looking through the third roll. I took the hint and ran through the rest of the film. Then I handed it back to Joe. 'You've got some nice shots there,' I said. 'Have you finished with the other one?' I asked Engles.

He handed it across to me. As he did so, he caught my eye. He was clearly excited. But he masked it by turning to Joe and beginning a long technical discussion on the merits of certain lighting and angles. And I was left wondering why a film shot of Valdini measuring a concrete wall should have aroused his interest.

8

We Dig Our Own Grave

It was a strange, tense lunch. Mayne sat apart from us at the opposite end of the table. He had searched our rooms, including Joe's. He knew none of us had a gun. But he took no chances. Hardly a word was spoken throughout the meal. Mayne was excited, though he tried not to show it. The rest of us were busy with our thoughts; all except Joe. He began to recall the few ski pictures that had been made. But he desisted when he found that Engles was not interested. 'What the hell's the matter with you all?' he demanded. 'And why's Mayne sitting up there as though he's suffering from a contagious disease?'

'Let it rest, Joe,' Engles said. 'We've had a row, that's all.'

'Oh. Valdini and the Contessa involved too?'

'Yes. They're feeding upstairs.'

He seemed satisfied with that and got on with his food in silence. It was difficult to believe that he did not even suspect that anything frightful had happened. Mayne became increasingly restless. He watched us all the time he was eating. I think he was afraid of us, even though we were unarmed. He watched us with cold, unemotional eyes. I remembered how Stelben had shot those men down. Here was another killer. As soon as he had got the gold, he would not hesitate to kill us. Joe might be safe as long as we could keep him in ignorance of the situation. But Engles and myself—he would most certainly destroy us. And what chance had we? It was like having lunch with the hangman on the day of one's execution. I began to feel sick.

The sweat broke out cold on my scalp, as though it were curry I was trying to eat. I pushed my plate away.

'Not feeling hungry, Blair?' Mayne asked.

'Would you, if you were me?' I replied sullenly.

'Perhaps not,' he said.

Joe looked across the table at me. 'What's the matter? Feeling ill, Neil?'

'No, I'm all right,' I said. But he wasn't convinced and went over to the bar and got me a drink. 'We'd better all have a drink,' he said. 'Might clear the air a bit.'

But it didn't. The liquor seemed cold and uninteresting and my mouth remained unpleasantly dry.

As soon as lunch was over, Joe got up and said, ''Fraid I'll have to tear myself away from this cheerful gathering.' And when nobody showed any desire for him to stay, he went back to his developing.

Mayne got up then and went upstairs. We heard the key turn in the lock of Valdini's room and the sound of his boots crossing to the window. Then the door shut and the key was turned in the lock again. When he came back into the room, he said, 'Now we can get started. Come with me, will you, Engles.'

Keramikos and I were left alone. We looked at each other. 'Can't we do something?' I said.

Keramikos shrugged his shoulders. 'It is difficult when you are dealing with a man who is armed and who will not hesitate to shoot. You might take up a chair and try to brain him as he comes in through the door again. Or you might throw a bottle at him and hope to stun him. Or again you might walk out through that door into the snow and try to get down to the bottom of the *slittovia*. For myself, I prefer to wait. Mayne is not the only one who has a gun. I took the precaution some time back of preparing for just such an eventuality. I have been in many difficult situations in my life. And I have discovered that always there is the moment. We shall see.' He was very pale and the lips of his small mouth were pressed close together so that they were the same colour as his skin.

'I'd rather take a chance than be shot like Stelben shot those men,' I said.

Again he shrugged his shoulders. He was not interested. I looked down the passage to the kitchen. There was no sign of Mayne. I glanced at the window facing the *slittovia*. Keramikos had his gun—but would he use it to assist us? I didn't trust him. My mind was suddenly made up. I crossed to the window and opened it. There was a deep bed of snow on the wooden platform below. And beyond the platform, the sleigh track, piled with drift snow, fell away into the murk of driving snow. 'Shut the window after me, will you,' I said to Keramikos.

'Do not be a fool, Blair,' he said as I climbed up on to the sill. 'He will see your tracks. It will do no good.'

But I ignored his advice. Anything was better than just waiting for the end. I stood up in the open window space and jumped. I landed quite softly. I was pitched forward on to my knees so that my face was buried in the snow. I raised my head and wiped the snow from my eyes. It was icy cold. I was facing straight down the sleigh track. I scrambled to my feet and plunged forward on to the track. The snow was thick for a bit and moved with me in a small avalanche, so that it was not unlike scree walking, which I had often done in the Lake District at home. But then I reached a patch where the snow had been blown clear of the track. My feet slipped from under me and I found myself sliding on my back. I must have fallen thirty feet or more before I fetched up in a bank of snow. I fought my way out of it and stood upright again.

There was a shout behind me. I glanced back and was surprised to see how near I still was to the hut. A ploughed-up track in the virgin snow showed the way I had come. A pistol shot cracked out and a bullet whipped into the snow just beside me. A voice called to me again. The words were lost in the roar of the wind through the trees. I turned and plunged on down the track.

No more bullets followed me. And, when next I looked back, the hut was no more than a vague, blurred shape. I began to feel excited. I was sheltered from the wind and, though I was already wet through, my exertions kept me warm.

I made steady progress now, sometimes wading through banks of deep snow, sometimes riding a moving sea of it, standing upright, and sometimes, in places where the track was clear, sliding down on my back.

I had just slid down one of these clear patches and nearly smothered myself in a deep drift, when I looked back. The hut had now completely disappeared from view, but coming out of the snow was the figure of a ski-er. He was taking the slope in quick zigzags. On the soft snow he did a jump turn and with his skis parallel to the slope, rode the snow as it spilled down as though he were surf-riding.

I dived for the shelter of the trees. The snow had drifted badly here. But wading and rolling, I made the side of the track, caught at a branch and pulled myself in amongst the trees.

I gave a quick glance back and was just in time to see Mayne do a perfect Christi against the deep snow through which I had struggled. He came up standing and facing me. Barely half-a-dozen yards separated us. I felt tears of anger smart in my eyes. My feet were bedded deep in snow and the branches of the trees were thick. Mayne slipped his hand inside his windbreaker and brought out his gun. 'Do I shoot you now?' he said. 'Or do you want to come back and join your friends?'

His voice was quite callous. It was clear that he did not mind whether he shot me now or later. 'All right,' I said. 'I'll come back.' I had no choice. But it was with a bitter sense of failure that I began to trudge back up the track I had made coming down. Once a drift gave way under me and I fell. I did not want to get up. I had a feeling of utter disappointment. But he began hacking at my ribs with the points of his skis. After that he gave me his sticks. He followed a little behind, side-stepping up, the gun ready in his hand.

I was utterly exhausted by the time I reached the top. He directed me round to the side of the concrete housing. I guessed that Engles and Keramikos were locked inside, for the door was being battered from within. Outside lay a pile of tools; picks, shovels and a heavy long-handled hammer that quarry men call a biddle. He unlocked the door and, catching hold of me by the back of the neck, flung me inside. I tripped on the snow in the doorway and fell. Something hit my head and I passed out.

When I came to, I found myself propped in a sitting position againt the wall. I was very cold and my eyes would not focus. I could not think where I was for the moment. There was a lot of noise and the room was full of dust. The blood hammered in my head, which felt heavy and painful. I put my hand up to my forehead. It was wet and sticky. My fingers came away covered in dirt and blood and the icy water of melted snow.

Then I remembered what had happened. I concentrated my gaze on the room. My back was resting in the corner of two walls. On the opposite side of the room, beyond the cable, Mayne stood with his back against the closed door. Under the switch-board, opposite the window, Engles and Keramikos were hacking away at the concrete flooring with pick and hammer. The room began to swim again. I closed my eyes.

When I opened them again, the room was steady. Engles had stopped pounding at the concrete with his hammer. He was leaning on the haft and wiping the sweat from his forehead. He caught my eye. 'Feeling better?' he asked.

'Yes,' I said. 'I'll be all right in a minute.'

But he saw I was shivering with cold and he said to Mayne, 'Why don't you lock him in his room? He's wet through. He'll get pneumonia.'

'That's his lookout,' was Mayne's reply. He did not trouble to conceal the fact that it would make no difference to me whether I caught pneumonia or not. But just at that moment I think I was past caring about death.

Engles looked across at me and then at Mayne. 'I don't often feel like killing people,' he said. 'But by God I do at the moment.'

'Better not try,' was all Mayne said.

Engles turned back and swung his hammer viciously against the concrete floor. The thud of it shook the whole room. They had moved the big cast-iron stove and where it had stood they were breaking up the concrete preparatory to digging. I glanced round the room. It was grey and dirty. The dust rose in a cloud round Engles and Keramikos—a fine, choking dust. Above me was the wall against which the German soldiers had been shot down. Examining it closely, I noticed that the concrete here was newer than the concrete of the floor.

I began to feel better. But my wet clothes chilled me and I was shivering uncontrollably. I got to my feet. I felt a bit dizzy, but otherwise not too bad. I said, 'Mind if I give you two a hand?' Engles turned. 'I'd be warmer doing some work,' I explained.

'No, come along,' he said.

Mayne made no objection and I climbed over the clutter of machinery. Already they had made a great gap in the concrete flooring. Keramikos was beginning to pick at the earth underneath. There was a hard frozen crust at the top, despite the concrete covering. But six inches down it was soft. Engles put his hammer down and I took up a pick. 'Take it easy,' Engles whispered to me. 'There's no hurry. Sorry you didn't make it. Good try—but quite hopeless.'

I nodded. 'It was foolish of me to try,' I said.

We worked in silence. Keramikos and Engles took up shovels and left me to pick the earth loose for them. Mayne gave us no rest. We worked steadily and methodically and all too quickly the hole deepened. 'We'll soon be on to the gold if this is where it is,' I whispered to Engles when our heads were bent close together.

The hole was over two feet deep already. 'He'll start shooting as soon as we get down to it, won't he?' I asked.

'Yes,' he said. 'But he'll have us get it all up first. That is, as you say, if it's here. How are you feeling now?'

'Cold,' I whispered back. 'But all right as long as I keep on the move.'

'Well, don't start anything until I tell you.' He bent close to Keramikos and began whispering to him. The Greek nodded and his thick hairy hands seemed to fasten more firmly round the haft of his shovel.

'Stop talking and get on with it,' Mayne ordered. His voice was cold, but he could not keep a tremor of excitement out of it.

'He begins to get excited now,' Keramikos said, his little eyes bright behind their lenses. 'Soon he will lose control. He will become obsessed by the gold. Then he may get careless. That will be our chance. Do not work too fast.' I wondered whether he had his gun on him.

'Stop talking!' Mayne's voice trembled. 'Work in silence or I'll shoot one of you.'

We worked in silence after that. But though we worked slowly, the hole steadily deepened. It began to get dark about four and Mayne switched on the light. It was a single naked bulb set in a wall socket beyond the switchboard. It was the same light that Holtz had smashed with his fist. Engles glanced at me. I think the same thought was in his mind, too. If I pretended to feel faint, could I get near enough to hit it with my pick, I wondered. 'Don't do anything foolish, Neil,' he whispered warningly.

I looked at Mayne. His eyes were bright. He was thinking of the gold. But they were watchful, too. The little black muzzle of the gun pointed straight at my stomach as our eyes met. 'If you move a step towards that light Blair, I'll blow your guts out for you,' he said.

We went on digging steadily. The three of us were taking turns at working actually in the hole now.

When it was some four feet deep Engles' shovel brought up a mouldy piece of cloth. Keramikos picked it off the pile of earth we had thrown up. 'This may interest you,' he said to Mayne. 'It is a piece of a German field uniform.'

'Get on digging,' was all Mayne said, but his eyes gleamed.

It was pretty unpleasant work after that. The bodies were half decayed. Only the bones were substantial. We pulled them out with our hands. It sickened me to see the remains of those men. Soon we should be no better off than they. We were digging our own grave.

There were rusty bayonets, guns with the butts and stocks rotten and the metal-work eaten away, webbing that fell to pieces as we pulled it out, and the bodies. Some of them had so little flesh left that they were scarcely more than skeletons draped in a mouldy covering that was part flesh, part clothing and part earth. We counted five in all, confirming Korporal Holtz's statement. Then our shovels uncovered the corner of a wooden box.

Keramikos, who was in the pit at the time, looked up at us. 'Pass it up,' Engles said. Keramikos bent down and scraped the earth away with his hands. I glanced at Mayne. He was very excited now. It showed in his eyes and in the tenseness of his body. But he did not move.

At last the box was completely exposed. It was about two feet long by a foot wide by six inches deep. The wood was dark and rotten and caked with earth. Keramikos got his hands under it and passed it up to Engles. It was heavy. He set it down beside the bodies and looked at Mayne.

'Get the rest up,' Mayne ordered.

'Wouldn't it be better to open it up?' Engles suggested.

Mayne hesitated. The lust to actually see the gold shone in his eyes. 'All right,' he said. 'Prise it open with that pick and let's have a look at it.'

Engles pushed the box along the concrete floor towards him. 'You'd better do it,' he said. 'It's your gold.'

Mayne laughed. 'I'm not a fool, Engles,' he said. 'Break it open!'

Engles shrugged his shoulders. He took up one of the picks and, setting his foot on the box to steady it, drove the point of the pick into it. It went in quite easily and when he put pressure on it, the rotten box fell apart.

It was full of earth.

Mayne uttered a cry and peered forward. Then he jumped back, the gun quivering in his hand. 'What sort of trick is this?' he screamed. 'What have you done with the gold, Engles? That's not gold. It's earth. What have you done with it?' He had lost control of himself completely. His face was twisted with rage. 'What have you done with it?' he repeated. 'Tell me what you've done with it, or—or—' He had become almost incoherent. For a moment I thought he was going to shoot Engles down.

'Don't be a fool,' Engles said. His voice was abrupt and had a ring of authority in it. 'Those boxes have lain there in the earth since they were put there. Your friends Muller and Mann probably know where the gold is. But you've killed them.'

'Why did you suggest opening the box?' Mayne demanded. He had got a grip on himself now. 'Why did you want me to see what was inside? You knew the gold wasn't there.'

'I only suspected that your friends had double-crossed you,' Engles replied.

'They wouldn't have done that. They told me everything as the price of their release from the Regina Coeli. They dug the hole for Stelben and stacked the boxes and the bodies round it. He locked himself in here after that and draped the window so that they couldn't see in. Later, when they were able to look in, the hole had been filled in, the floor cemented over and the stove put back in its place. They weren't able to get inside because the door was locked.'

'That's their story,' Engles said.

Mayne looked wildly round the room. 'It's in here somewhere,' he said. 'It must be.'

'Are you sure Muller and Mann really brought it in here?' Engles asked quietly.

'Yes, of course they did. And he couldn't have shifted it out of this room without their knowing.'

'You've only got their word for it,' Engles reminded him. 'After all, you double-crossed them. No reason why they shouldn't have double-crossed you.'

'Get up the rest of the boxes,' Mayne ordered.

'If one box is full of earth, the others will be,' said Keramikos.

'Get them up,' Mayne snarled.

We worked much faster now. We got up twenty-one boxes. Each one, as we got it up, was split open. And each one was full of earth.

'What do you wish us to do now?' Keramikos asked as the last one was split open to reveal its unprofitable contents.

But Mayne was not listening. His eyes roved over the machinery, the switchboard and the walls. 'It's in here somewhere,' he said. 'I'm certain of it. And I'll find it if I have to tear the place to pieces.'

'Suppose we have a drink and consider the matter?' Engles suggested.

Mayne looked at him. He hesitated. He had lost his self-confidence. 'All right,' he said. His voice was toneless. 'Put those things back in the hole and fill it in.' He indicated the bodies dumped on top of the earth in a grotesque pile.

When we had roughly filled in the hole, we carried the tools back to the hut. The snow seemed to be slackening, but it was bitterly cold and the wind drove right through my wet clothes. Joe was sitting snugly by the stove, reading. 'What in God's name have you people been up to now?' he asked. 'I was getting worried. What have you been doing with those things—gardening?' He indicated the tools we were carrying.

'No. Digging for gold,' Engles answered.

Joe grunted. 'You look as though you'd been examining the sewage system.'

Mayne went upstairs. Joe got up from his chair. 'This is a hell of a crazy place,' he said. His words were directed at Engles. 'First you say there's been a row between you and Mayne. Then you disappear with him, the whole gang of you. Valdini and the Contessa shut themselves up in their room. Suppose you tell me just what is going on.'

Engles said, 'Sit down and relax, Joe. You're paid as a cameraman, not as a nursemaid.'

'Yes, but this is ridiculous, old man,' he persisted. 'Something is going on here—'

'Are you a cameraman or not?' Engles' voice was suddenly sharp.

'Of course I'm a cameraman.' Joe's tone was aggrieved.

'Well, get on with your job, then. I'm not here to run around with you. You missed some good shots this afternoon because you were lazy and didn't get out.'

'Yes, but—'

'Good God, man, do you want me to wet nurse you on your job?'

Joe subsided sullenly back into his book. It was unkind and unfair. But it silenced his questions. The three of us went through to the back of the hut and put the tools in the ski room. As we stacked them in the corner, Keramikos said, 'I think Mayne will wish for terms now. He does not like being alone. And now that he does not know where the gold is, he will be unhappy. He does not dare shoot us because we may know where it is. But also he does not dare let us live unless we are his partners. I think he would like us all to be partners now.'

'But should we agree?' I asked him. 'With your help we should be able to dispose of him.' I was thinking of the gun he had.

Keramikos shook his head. 'No, no. He may be useful. We do not know how much he knows. We should come to terms first.'

'But does he know where the gold is any more than we do?' Engles asked.

Keramikos shrugged. 'Four heads are always better than one, my friend,' he replied non-commitally.

We went upstairs then. I was glad to get out of my cold clothes and change into something warm. Engles came into my room as soon as he was cleaned up. 'How are you feeling, Neil?'

'Not too bad,' I told him.

'Better have some Elastoplast on that cut of yours,' he said. 'I've got some in my haversack.'

He returned a moment later and put a strip of plaster on it. 'There,' he said, patting my shoulder. 'It's only a surface cut and a bit of bruising. Sorry it didn't come off, that break for freedom of yours. It was a good try.'

'It was rather a futile effort,' I apologised.

'Unnecessary, shall we say.' He grinned cheerfully. 'Still you weren't to know that.'

'You mean, you knew the gold wouldn't be in those boxes?' I asked.

'Shall we say I had a shrewd suspicion.' He lit a cigarette and as he watched the flame of the match die out, he said, 'The man we need to watch now is our friend Keramikos. He is a much more subtle character than Mayne. And he thinks that we know where the gold is.'

'And—do we?' I asked.

He smiled then. 'The less you know about it the better,' he replied good-humouredly. 'Come down and have a drink. We're going to get plastered tonight. And see that you get as drunk as I do.'

It was a macabre sort of evening. Engles was at his wittiest, telling anecdote after anecdote of film stars he had known, directors he had got the better of, cocktail parties that had ended in rows. He worked like a street vendor to spread a veneer of cheerfulness over his audience. At first the audience was myself only. But then he brought Joe out of his Western and smoothed his ruffled feathers. And when Keramikos joined us, there was only Mayne left outside the little group by the bar.

That was what Engles had been playing for. Mayne went over to the piano and bull-dozed his way through a sonorous piece of Bach. It was a vicious piece of playing. The old piano cried aloud his mood of frustration and impotent anger.

And Engles talked through it until he had us all roaring with laughter. It was a forced gaiety in that it was produced intentionally by wit and cognac. But the laughter was real. And that was what eventually got Mayne. It took away his authority. It undermined his confidence. He wasn't sure of himself now that he had failed to find the gold. With a gun in his hand and everybody doing what they were told, he could still have bolstered up his self-esteem. But to be ignored! To see the rest of us in such apparently hilarious spirits. It was too much for him. He suddenly crashed his hands on to the keys and stood up. 'Stop laughing!' he shouted.

'Ignore him,' Engles whispered. And he went on talking. We began to laugh again.

'Stop it, do you hear?'

Engles turned. He was swaying slightly. 'S–shtop what, sir?' he asked blandly.

'Go and sit down by the fire and stop that noise,' Mayne ordered.

'What noise? Do you hear a noise, Neil?' He turned in a dignified manner to Mayne. 'No noise here, old man. Must be the piano.'

I glanced at Mayne this time. He was white with anger. But he hesitated. He didn't know what line to take. 'Engles!' he said. 'Go and sit down.'

'Oh, go to hell!' was all the reply he got.

His hand went to the pocket where his gun was. But he stopped. He stood there for a moment, looking at us and biting his lip. Then he sat down at the piano again.

Shortly after this Anna came in with the dinner things. Engles looked at the three of us. 'Don't want any food, do we? I don't mind, eat if you want to. But I'm all for keeping straight on drinking. Or suppose we have it on the bar? Then those who want it can pick at it.' And he gave instructions to Anna to put the food on the bar.

That was the last straw. Mayne either had to get Anna to bring him his food separately or to come over and join us at the bar. He chose the latter course. And shortly after that, he drew Engles on one side. Keramikos was then called over to join them. The consultation lasted only a few minutes. Then the three of them shook hands. I heard Engles say, 'I think you're being very sensible, Mayne.'

Mayne went behind the bar then and began to produce a special mixture of his own for us to try. As he stooped to get a bottle, Engles leaned towards me. 'No shooting. Three-way split.' And his eyelid flickered with amusement.

'What about Carla?' I whispered.

'No provision made,' he replied.

Mayne straightened up and began to mix the drinks, using an empty bottle as a shaker. His ease of manner had partly returned. To see him standing there, smiling and talking and busying himself about our drinks, you would have thought him a charming host—possibly a wealthy play-boy, perhaps an actor, maybe even an artist, but never a ruthless, cold-blooded killer.

And why did we all drink so much at the bar that night? Each of us had a different reason. Engles set the pace— unobtrusively, of course, but nevertheless he set the pace. And he made it fast, because he wished to appear to be drunk and he wanted the others to be drunk. I drank because the liquor warmed me and I was keeping Engles company. Joe drank because everyone was friends again and that pleased him. He hated emotional conflicts. No doubt that was why he was a bachelor. Mayne drank because he wanted to catch up with the spirits of the party and to forget that moment at the piano. And Keramikos? I wasn't sure at the time why Keramikos drank.

Engles seemed to get drunk quicker than the others. By eleven o'clock he had had a row with Joe and staggered out of the bar in a blazing temper. Keramikos made a clumsy movement to take up his glass and knocked it on to the floor. He looked at it for a second in a fuddled way, took off his glasses and wiped his eyes and then walked stiffly to the door and went up to bed. The party was beginning to break up. I followed shortly afterwards, leaving Mayne and Joe, both very tight. When I got upstairs, I found Engles sitting on my bed. 'I take it you're not as drunk as you appear to be?' he said.

'I'm pleasantly happy,' I said. 'But I could doubtless sober up if you could show me any good reason why I should.'

'We're getting out of here,' he said.

'When?' I asked.

'Tonight,' he replied. 'As soon as everybody has settled down.' I noticed then that he had got his ski boots on and his windbreaker and gloves were on the chair beside the bed. 'Lock the door,' he said, 'and come in and sit down.'

When I had done this, he began to give me instructions. He was concise and clear, just as he had always been when briefing us before an action. His manner was calm and he chose his words carefully, though he was speaking fast. How he managed to think so clearly after all the liquor he had drunk, I don't know. But then, as I have said, he took drink like most people take food. It seemed to feed his brain and stimulate his mind. For myself, I felt distinctly light-headed and I had to concentrate hard to follow and remember what he was saying.

'Have you looked outside?' he asked me.

I told him, 'No.'

'Pull back that curtain, then, and have a look.'

I did this and was surprised to see that it had stopped snowing and the sky had cleared. The great banks of fresh snow that were piled up round the hut shone white in bright moonlight. But the wind still howled dismally and, wherever I looked, the powdery top layer of snow was moving in the way that fine sand shifts low across the desert before a sandstorm.

'There's a good, deep drift of snow just below the window here,' he went on. 'As soon as everybody has settled down for the night, I'm going to drop out of your window on to the belvedere. You probably didn't notice, but when we came up to the hut with those tools this evening, I dropped one of the picks into a drift. Mayne didn't notice either. I'm going to take that pick, go through under the supports of the hut and smash open the door to the cable machine-room. Unfortunately Keramikos' room is just above it. He'll hear me breaking in the door and he'll come after me then. I don't think I'll have time to smash the other skis. Keramikos has a gun. He told me that in the machine-room this afternoon and I don't want to get shot before I'm clear of this place.'

'I know he's got a gun,' I said. 'But he's too drunk to use it.'

Engles gave a short laugh. 'Nonsense,' he said. 'Keramikos is as sober as I am. And he knows that I can't do him any harm at the moment unless I get at those skis.'

'You mean he was pretending to be drunk?' I asked. My brain was working very slowly.

Engles nodded. 'That last drink I mixed—he didn't touch it. And I didn't give it to you or Joe. There was a Micky in it. He knew it as soon as he tasted it. Mayne was the only one who drank it. He'll sleep all right tonight.'

'But I don't quite see why Keramikos should want to follow you,' I said.

'My God! You're dull tonight, Neil,' said Engles sharply. 'Keramikos is a Greek national. In Greece we couldn't touch him. But here in Italy it's different. Italy is still conquered territory. We still have our troops in Venezia Giulia. If I could get through to the Field Security Police there, he'd have a pretty nasty time getting out of the country. And he knows that I'm more interested in him than in the gold.'

He lit a cigarette. 'Now then, this is what I want you to do, Neil,' he went on. 'As soon as I have dropped through this window, I want you to open your door slightly and watch the corridor. When Keramikos comes out of his room, slip into Joe's room. Don't let Keramikos see you though. The window of Joe's room faces the *slittovia*. Lean out and lob something heavy, like the water jug, down by the doorway of the machine-room. I'll know then what margin of time I have. My tracks will be perfectly clear to him. I'll take the slalom run down to Tre Croci. I'll go straight across the pass on to the old Military Patrol route up to Tondi di Faloria. I'll take him through what our boys used to call the 'Gun Barrel,' and so down to the *carabinieri* post at Cortina. As soon as Keramikos leaves on my trail, I want you to drop on to the belvedere, get your skis out and make for the hotel at Tre Croci. Get on the phone then to Trieste—Major Musgrave of the Field Security Police. Tell him you're speaking for me. He knows who I am. Tell him to send me as many men as he can from the nearest section by jeep. They're to meet me at the *carabinieri* post in Cortina. Tell him as much as is necessary to impress on him the urgency of the matter. Make it clear to him that there's a Nazi agent to be picked up. And they must come up by jeep. Tell him the snow is thick and they may not be able to get through in a larger vehicle.' He stopped then and looked at me closely. 'Now, are those instructions quite clear, Neil?'

I nodded. 'Perfectly clear,' I assured him. The thought of action had sobered me up.

But he wasn't satisfied. He had me repeat them over to him. When I had finished, he lay back on the bed and drew a blanket over himself. 'Now sit there and listen for the others to come to bed,' he said. 'Who's still down there—Joe and Mayne? Right. Wake me half an hour after the last of them has come to bed. And don't fall asleep.'

'I won't,' I said.

'One other thing,' he added as he settled himself. 'If you can't get through to Trieste, try Udine or any town where we've got troops and persuade the garrison commander to take action. I don't want Keramikos to slip through our fingers. He did us a lot of damage in Greece and he's probably hand-in-glove with ELAS.'

'Don't worry,' I said. 'I'll get through to someone.'

'Good!' he said. And within a few minutes he was asleep. He was like that—always able to sleep when he wanted to.

It must have been about half an hour later that Joe and Mayne came up together. They sounded talkative and drunk. Their footsteps stopped at the head of the stairs by Mayne's door. It was Mayne who was talking and the touch of Irish brogue in his speech was more pronounced than usual. At length they wished each other good-night. Mayne's door closed. Joe's footsteps wavered along the corridor. He went into his room and I heard him sit down on his bed with a grunt. He remained there for some time. At length he began to move about again. Then the springs of the bed creaked. He grunted for a moment as he settled himself and then began to snore. I glanced at my watch. It was just after midnight.

I got up then and, unlocking the door, opened it a fraction. The naked electric light bulb burned in the corridor. The stairs were a dark pit. All was very silent. I closed the door and sat down in my chair again. I began to feel sleepy. I kept on glancing at my watch. The minutes ticked by incredibly slowly.

But at last the half-hour was up and I woke Engles. He looked at his watch and was wide awake in the instant. 'Thanks,' he said and put on his windbreaker and gloves. Then he opened the little casement window and, supporting himself on a chair, began to wriggle through, feet first. When all but his head and shoulders were through and he was supporting himself on his elbows he said, 'Stick by the telephone at Tre Croci, will you, Neil. I'll ring you there as soon as I get into Cortina.'

'I will,' I said. 'Good luck!'

He nodded and dropped from sight.

I looked out of the window then and saw him sprawled in a drift of snow. He got to his feet and waded through the snow to one of the tables. He felt about in the snow and pulled out the pick he had dropped. He looked up then and raised his hand. His face looked white and set in the moonlight. He crossed the belvedere and disappeared from sight round the back of the hut.

I set my door ajar and looked down the length of the corridor. And at that moment Aldo popped his head out of Valdini's old room. It shone baldly in the naked light. He looked like a clown as he peered quickly left and right along the corridor. Then he slipped out and vanished into the black void of the staircase on stockinged feet.

9

Col Da Varda in Flames

Having seen Aldo come out of the room in which Carla was imprisoned, I half expected her to emerge at any moment. But the corridor remained empty. It seemed a long time that I remained there with my eye to the crack through which a cold draught came. But it was only three minutes by my watch before the second door from the end was suddenly thrown open and Keramikos rushed out. He was fully clothed even to ski boots which clattered noisily on the boards as he dived down the stairs.

As soon as he was out of sight, I went into Joe's room. The noise had not wakened him. He was snoring peacefully, his face to the wall and his mouth open. I flung open the window and leaned out with the water jug in my hand. The façade of the hut was brilliantly lit in the moonlight. I swung the jug with my arm straight and pitched it just beyond the machine-room so that Engles could not fail to see it from the doorway.

He appeared at once. He had his skis on, but he did not leave at once. He came round to the front of the concrete housing and slipped his right ski along the wall, for all the world as though he were measuring the frontage as Valdini had done. Then he turned quickly and, with a flick of his sticks, he was off down the slalom run. A shot rang out from beneath the hut. I stayed at the window, keeping an eye on my watch, the second-hand of which was quite visible in the moonlight. Just eighty-five seconds after Engles had disappeared into the dark band of the trees, Keramikos started down the slalom run after him. And from the speed at which he took the first slope and the way he handled his sticks, I guessed him to be a pretty good ski-er.

I closed the window then. Joe hadn't stirred. I opened his door and glanced quickly out to see whether the corridor was clear. And at that moment Carla's head appeared—not out of the door of Valdini's room, but up the stairs. She was carrying a heavy can. I pulled my head back then and listened, waiting for her to go back into Valdini's room.

A board creaked. There was silence for a moment. Then I heard the burble of liquid being poured out of a can. It was the sound a petrol can makes whilst being emptied. I took a chance on her seeing me and looked out. She was bent low, pouring liquid from the can on to the floor outside Mayne's door. It was petrol. I could smell it, even though I was at the opposite end of the corridor. And as I realised this, I knew what she was going to do.

I stepped out into the corridor then. She looked up at the sound of my slippers on the boards, but she did not stop pouring. The liquid was streaming under the door of Mayne's room. 'Don't be a fool!' I said. 'You can't do that.'

She laid the can on its side and straightened herself. She had a box of matches in her hand. Her face looked white and strained and there were dark bruises on either side of her mouth where a gag had been. She didn't seem very steady, for she leaned against the wall for support. Her eyes stared at me wildly down the length of the corridor. 'I cannot—no?' She fumbled for a match and backed to the stairs. Then she struck it viciously and held it up. 'Then you watch,' she said. And she tossed the burning match lightly into the pool of petrol. It went up with a roar. In an instant the whole far end of the corridor was a sheet of flame.

Carla had disappeared down the stairs. I dived back into Joe's room and dragged him from his bed. 'Go away,' he grunted as he hit the floor. 'Not the time for damn-fool tricks. Oh, my head!'

I slapped him across the face. 'Wake up!' I shouted at him. 'The place is on fire.'

'Uh?' He opened his eyes and shook his head so that his cheeks quivered. 'Wadidyousay?'

'Fire!' I yelled at him.

'Eh? What?' He sat up and regarded me with bleary eyes. 'Aren't trying to be funny by any chance, old man?'

'For God's sake!' I said. 'Can't you hear it?'

'There's a sort of roaring in my ears. Blood pressure. Always get it after drinking too much.' Then he suddenly began sniffing. 'By God! You're right. There is a fire.'

He lumbered awkwardly to his feet, shaking himself like a bear coming out of hibernation. 'Bad thing, drink,' he muttered. 'Perhaps it's all a dream?'

'It isn't a dream,' I said. 'Go and look for yourself.' I began gathering up his clothes.

As soon as he opened the door a blast of hot air hit us in the face. There was not much smoke. The wood had caught now and the flames were roaring and crackling along the match-boarding. 'Good God!' Joe said. 'Place'll burn like tinder.'

'Come through into my room,' I said. 'The drop on to the belvedere isn't so great there.'

He followed me, trailing a bundle of hastily gathered clothes in his arms. He had slung his small camera round his neck. We pitched everything out of the window. I tossed my typewriter out and saw it landed safely in soft snow. Then I helped Joe through the window. It was a close thing. His heavy bulk could only just squeeze through. When he was half-way through, he suddenly looked at me. 'Where's Engles?' he asked. He had sobered up a lot.

'He's all right,' I said. 'He's gone off with Keramikos.'

'And the others?'

'I think Mayne is trapped,' I said. 'But he should be able to make it through the window.'

'Uh. Reminds me of the things they used to make us do on Sports Day—you know, under the tarpaulin, through the wire

158

and along the sewage piping. Thank God I haven't got to eat an apple on the end of a string at the finish.'

'No, but you've got to put your clothes on out there in the snow,' I said. 'That should be funny enough for you.'

'My God!' he said. 'My cameras!'

'Where are they?'

'Out the back. I should be able to get to them all right.' But the thought seemed to spur him on and a moment later, puffing and blowing, he disappeared from sight. I leaned out of the window and saw the huge blue bulk of his pyjamas shamble off through the snow in search of his clothes. Then I, too, got my legs through that window. Though the door was shut, the room was getting very hot and smoke was coiling in around the edges of the door in grey wisps.

I landed quite softly and, as I scrambled to my feet, the report of a gun nearly deafened me. I span round. Carla was standing on the belvedere, leaning over the wooden rail so that she could see along the front of the hut. She had a sporting piece in her hands—about a twelve bore—and smoke was curling up from one of the twin barrels. Her scarlet ski suit stood out like a smear of blood against the white background. She broke the piece and reloaded with a cartridge from her pocket. As she snapped back the breech, she noticed me. 'You stay away,' she said. 'This is not your business.' The gun was pointed at me for a moment. She was like a jungle cat defending her young. Her eyes still had that wild look. She was beyond reason—in the grip of a kind of madness.

Her eyes quickly strayed from me back along the front of the building. She turned suddenly and waded through the snow to the steps. Then she disappeared from view.

I crossed to the rail and leaned over. She was making her way slowly along the front of the building towards the top of the *slittovia*, her head back so that she looked up to where the glow of the flames showed red in the farthest bedroom window.

Mayne's head appeared at the window. There was a stab of flame as he fired. The scarlet ski suit was jerked back suddenly like a puppet on a string. It turned slightly and sagged. But it fetched up in a sitting position in the snow and raised the gun. There was a blast of red-and-yellow fire, the crash of a shot and Mayne's head was withdrawn. He fired at her twice after that as she sat huddled in the snow. The second time Carla did not reply.

A moment later Mayne's legs appeared through the window. They were picked out quite plainly in the glow of the flames. Carla slowly raised her gun and fired both barrels. The distance was only a matter of some forty feet. There was a horrible scream of agony. The legs writhed convulsively and were withdrawn. Carla slowly broke the piece and reloaded. The flames brightened suddenly inside the bedroom and then burned red. The glow seemed to sweep right up to the glass of the window and then a great tongue of flame licked up out of the casement, hissing as it turned the snow that hung from the roof to steam. The white icing of snow that covered the roof seemed to draw back from the flames. It wilted visibly. A piece of the gabling fell in. A great column of steam rose hissing towards the cold curtain of the stars. A gout of flame followed it through the gaping rent in the roof. The trees glowed warmly and the snow all round the hut was coloured a gay pink.

Mayne's head suddenly appeared again amidst the flames at the window. He fired three times at Carla. The little stabbing flames of his gun were hardly visible in the glare. Carla fired one barrel. That was all. Then she rolled over and buried her face in the snow.

Mayne dropped his gun. He was pulling at the window frame, trying to drag himself out. He appeared to be wounded. When he was half-out, his stomach supporting him on the window sill, he began to scream. It was a horrible sound—very animal and very high pitched. A draught had been created by the hole in the gable roofing and a great wave of flame rolled over him and roared up out of the window. I saw his hair catch fire. It burned like a piece of furze. The skin of his face blackened.

He gave a convulsive, agonised heave with his hands and fell head first from the window, a human torch, his whole body blazing furiously. He hit a drift of snow beyond the *slittovia* platform. A cloud of steam rose from the spot. The flames were instantly extinguished. A great black hole was burned in the snow.

'The poor devil!' Joe said. He was standing beside me, half-dressed. 'Is that damned Contessa of yours mad?'

'I think she's dead,' I said. 'Finish putting on your clothes. I'll go and see if there's anything we can do.'

Another piece of the roofing went as I made my way to the head of the *slittovia*. Sparks and steam rose high into the night and were whipped away by the wind. Carla's body was huddled in the snow close to the platform at the top of the sleigh track. It was quite still. The scarlet of her ski suit glowed brightly in the lurid light. I turned her over. Her eyes stared wide out of a face covered in wet snow. There was a patch of blood in the hollow her body had made in the snow. A bullet had shattered her shoulder. Two more had struck her in the chest. The stains were a darker red than her ski suit. She was dead.

I crossed the platform then and made for the dark hole where Mayne had fallen. His body lay right below the spot where the fire was fiercest. Great gouts of flame were licking through the broken gabling. The wind was driving the fire through the wooden building, fanning the flames so that they looked like the exotic petals of some fearful jungle flower, writhing in horrid carnivorous ecstasy. One glance at Mayne told me that there was nothing to be done for him. His body was a charred and blackened mass, lying in a pool of melted snow. It was twisted and unnatural. And where the clothing had fallen away from one arm, the unburned flesh was pock-marked with shot. His had been an unpleasant death.

Joe joined me then. 'Dead?' he asked.

I nodded. 'Nothing we can do. Better go and get your cameras. I'll give you a hand.'

Joe did not move. He was staring up at the flaming building. There was a crash. The whole gable that had roofed Mayne's room seemed to crumple. We scrambled back through the snow just in time. It collapsed with a roar. The flames licked round this fresh wound with increasing fury. Sparks flew and were driven into the night. A set of beams, charred and eaten by the fire and still blazing, fell across Mayne's body. They stood for a second, up-ended in the snow. Then they keeled over against the side of the building, their bases hissing and blackened, the upper ends still flaming. The wood of the hut flooring caught and began to burn. 'Better hurry, Joe,' I said.

But all he said was, 'Christ! What a film shot!'

'What about Aldo and his wife, and Anna?' I said, shaking his arm.

'Eh? Oh, they live downstairs. They'll be all right.'

We found them round the back, dragging their belongings out into the snow. At least, the two women were. Aldo was wandering about helplessly, wringing his hands and muttering, '*Mamma mia! Mamma mia!*' I imagine he felt pretty sick at having helped Carla to escape.

We got Joe's gear out and dumped it in the snow. It was whilst I was doing this that I suddenly remembered the skis. Without them it would take me hours to get down to Tre Croci. I stumbled round to the front of the building again. My heart sank at the sight of it. The whole front was ablaze now. Half the roof was gone and where the staircase had been the upper storey was nothing more than gaunt, blackened beams pointing flaming fingers at the moon. The door of the machine-room stood open as Engles and Keramikos had left it. It was already blackened with the heat and beginning to smoulder. The flooring above the concrete room was alight and the supports all round it flaming. At any moment the whole structure might collapse on top of it.

I rolled quickly in the heat-thawed snow till my clothes were sodden. Then, with a wet handkerchief tied round my face, I sloshed through the melting snow and in through the black, gaping doorway. The inside of that concrete room was like an oven. It was full of smoke. I couldn't see a thing. I stumbled over the pick Engles had used to batter in the door and felt my way to the corner where we had put the skis. Several fell as I touched them. But the clatter they made was scarcely audible above the roar of the flames overhead. I felt along the warm concrete wall with my hands and found a bundle still tied together. With these over my shoulder, I stumbled through the red gap of the doorway, out through the blazing pine supports and into the cold, sodden snow.

I set the skis down, points upwards, in a drift and looked back at the blaze. As I did so, one of the pine supports near the entrance to the machine-room splintered and flared. The blazing floor above it sagged dangerously. A moment later several supports gave with loud cracks and a burst of flame. The flooring, which they supported, slowly buckled, and then the whole blazing façade above folded inwards and sank with a roar of flame and broken wood. Myriad sparks rushed into the night and the flames roared up through the gap in a solid sheet.

Joe came round the end of the building then. I beckoned to him and began to unfasten the skis. When he came up, he said, 'How did this fire start, Neil?'

'Petrol,' I said, fastening on a pair of skis. 'Carla set light to it.'

'Good Lord! Whatever for?'

'Revenge,' I told him. 'Mayne had double-crossed her and jilted her. He'd also planned to murder her.'

He stared at me. 'Are you making this up?' he asked. 'Where's Valdini?'

'Mayne shot him,' I said. I had finished putting on the skis. I straightened up then and found Joe's face a picture of incredulity in the ruddy glare. 'I've got to get down to Tre Croci,' I told him. 'I must get to a phone. I'll take the slalom run. Will you follow me? I'll tell you all about it down at the hotel.' I did not wait for his reply. I put my hands through the leather thongs of the sticks and started off across the snow.

The slalom wasn't an easy run. It was very steep, following pretty much the line of the *slittovia*, snaking down almost parallel to it. I took it as slowly as possible, but the fresh snow was deep and I was only able to break my speed by snow-ploughing in places. Stem turns were difficult and I often had to brake by running into the soft snow at the side of the run or by falling.

After the lurid light and the roar of the flames at the hut, it was strangely dark and silent going down through the woods. Moonlight filtered through the feathery web of the pine branches and the only sounds were the wind whipping the topmost branches and the hiss of my skis through the snow.

I suppose it took me about half an hour to get down that run. It seemed much longer, for my ski suit was wet through and it was very cold. But my watch showed the time to be only one forty-five as I passed the hut where Emilio lived at the bottom of the *slittovia*. I looked up the long white avenue of the cable track gleaming brightly in the moonlight. At the top, the white of the snow seemed to blossom into a great, violent mushroom of fire. It was no longer possible to discern the shape of the hut. It was just a flaming mass, white at the centre, fading to a dull orange at the edges and throwing out a great trailer of sparks and smoke, so that it looked like a meteor rushing through the night.

When I reached the hotel I found everybody up and bustling to form a party to go up and fight the flames. I was immediately surrounded by an excited crowd, all dressed in their ski clothes. I asked for the manager. He came fussing through the group round me, a stout, important-looking little man with a sallow, worried face and lank, oily hair. 'You all right, *signore*? Are there any hurt?'

I told him the fire had hurt no one, that it was quite beyond control and would soon burn itself out. Then I asked if I could use his office and his telephone. 'But of course, *signore*. Anything I can do, you have but to command.' He put two electric fires on for me, had a waiter bring me a drink and a change of clothing and had a hot meal conjured for me out of the kitchen, all in an instant. It was a big moment for him. He was showing his guests how good and generous a host he was. He nearly drove me frantic with his constant enquiries after my health. And all the while I had the telephone pressed to my ear. I spoke to Bologna, Mestre, Milan. Once a line was crossed and it was Rome talking to me. But Trieste or Udine—no.

Joe came puffing in just as I was talking to Bologna for the third time. He looked as though he had had a lot of falls. He was wet with snow and flopped exhausted into an arm-chair. He had his baby camera still slung round his neck. He gave the little manager fresh scope. Brandy was rushed to the scene. He was stripped of his ski suit and swathed in a monstrosity of a dressing-gown decked with purple-and-orange stripes. More food was brought. And whilst all this was going on and in the intervals of my telephonic tour of the main exchanges of Italy, I tried to give him some idea of what had been happening up at Col da Varda. I did not mention the gold, and this omission left loopholes in the story, so that I do not think he really believed it all.

But in the midst of his questions, Trieste suddenly asked me why I did not answer. I asked for the military exchange and got through to Major Musgrave at his hotel. His voice barked at me sleepily down the line. But annoyance changed to interest as I mentioned Engles' name and told him what I wanted. 'Right-ho,' was the reply, thin and faint as though at a great distance. 'I'll ring Udine and have 'em move off at once. The *carabinieri* post at Cortina, you say? Okay. Tell Derek they ought to be there about nine-ish, unless the road is blocked.' It was all settled in a matter of a few minutes, and I put the phone down with a sigh of relief.

The little manager had exhausted himself by then. Everyone had gone back to bed. I looked out into the hall. The hotel was quiet again. The porter slept, curled up in a chair by the stove. A big clock ticked solemnly below the staircase. It was ten past four. I went back into the office. Joe was asleep in the arm-chair, snoring gently. I pulled the heavy curtains aside and peered out. The moon was setting in a great yellow ball behind the shoulder of Monte Cristallo. The stars were brighter, the sky darker. Only the faintest glow showed at the top of the *slittovia*. The fire was burning itself out. I pulled a chair up to one of the electric heaters and settled myself down to await Engles' phone call.

I suppose I must have dozed off, for I don't remember the passage of time and it must have been after six when I was woken by the sound of voices in the hall. Then the door of the room was thrown open and Engles staggered in.

I remember I started to my feet. I hadn't expected him. His face was white and haggard. His ski suit was torn. There was blood on the front of his wind-breaker, and a great red stain just above the left groin. 'Get through to Trieste?' he asked. His voice sounded thin and exhausted.

'Yes,' I said. 'They'll be at the *carabinieri* post about nine.'

Engles gave a wry smile. 'Won't be necessary.' He stumbled over to the desk and collapsed into the leather-padded swivel-chair. 'Keramikos is dead,' he added.

'What happened?' I asked.

He stared vacantly at the typewriter that stood on the polished mahogany. He lurched slowly forward and removed the cover. Then he pulled the typewriter close to him and inserted a sheet of paper. 'Give me a cigarette,' he said. I put one in his mouth and lit it for him. He didn't speak for a moment. He just sat there with the cigarette dangling from the corner of his mouth and his eyes fixed on the blank sheet of paper in the typewriter. 'My God!' he said slowly. 'What a story! It'll make film history. A thriller that really happened. It's never been done before—not like this.' His eyes were alight with the old enthusiasm. His fingers strayed to the keys and he began to type.

Joe woke with a grunt at the sound of the typewriter and stared at Engles with his mouth open, as though he had seen a ghost.

I watched over Engles' shoulder. He wrote:

THE LONELY SKI-ER

SCENARIO OF A THRILLER THAT REALLY HAPPENED

The click of the keys slowed and faltered. The cigarette dropped from his lips and lay on his lap, burning a brown mark on the white of his ski suit. His teeth were grinding together and beads of sweat glistened on his forehead. He raised his fingers to the keyboard again and added another line:

by Neil Blair

He stopped then and stared at it with a little smile. A froth of blood bubbled at his lips. His wrists went slack so that the fingers raised a jumble of type arms. Then he gently keeled over and slipped to the floor before I could catch him.

When we picked him up, he was dead.

10

The Lonely Skier

I was filled with a bitter hatred for that gold as I looked down at Engles' body, sprawled limp in the easy-chair in which we had placed it.

What was there in gold? Little bricks of a particularly useless metal—no more. It had no intrinsic value, save that its rarity made it suitable for use as a means of exchange. Yet, though inanimate, it seemed to have a deadly personality of its own. It could draw men from the ends of the earth in search of it. It was like a magnet—and all it attracted was greed. The story of Midas had shown men its uselessness. Yet throughout history, ever since the yellow metal had first been discovered, men had killed each other in the scramble to obtain it. They had subjected thousands to the lingering death of phthisis to drag it from deep mine shafts, from places as far apart as Alaska and the Klondyke. And others had dedicated their lives to a hard gamble in useful products in order to procure it and store it back in underground vaults.

To get hold of this particular little pile of gold, Stelben had slaughtered nine men. And after his death, though the gold was buried in the heart of the Dolomites, it had attracted a group of people from different parts of Europe to squabble and kill each other over it.

Of all the people whom it had drawn up the *slittovia* to Col da Varda, I was the only one left alive. They had not been a particularly attractive group of characters: Stefan Valdini, gangster and procurer; Carla Rometta, a crook and little better than a common prostitute; Gilbert Mayne, *alias* Stuart Ross, deserter, gangster and killer; Keramikos, a Nazi agent with Greek nationality. They had all died because of that gold.

And now—Derek Engles.

He had had his faults. But he had been a brilliant and attractive personality. He might have been one of the great of the film world. And now all that remained of him was a body sprawled lifeless in an easy-chair in a mountain hotel in Italy. He would never direct another film. He had even had to pass on to me the responsibility for telling the story of Col da Varda.

Joe was leaning over the body, ripping the clothing away from the wound in the groin. 'Doesn't look like a bullet,' he said as he laid bare the white skin of the stomach.

I peered over his shoulder. It was more a bruise than a wound. The skin seemed to have been burst open in an irregular, ragged tear. The flesh round it was horribly bruised.

Joe shook his head. 'Something hit him there—and hit him hard.' He examined the rest of the body. There was no sign of any other wound. He straightened up with a grunt. 'He must have known he was dying when he came in,' he said. 'No one could have an injury like that and not know he was finished. I wonder how far away from here it happened. Every step afterwards must have been agony.' He walked to the window and looked out. 'Clouding over, Neil,' he said, letting the curtain drop again. 'If it begins to snow again his tracks will be covered up and we'll never know how it happened.'

'You mean that we ought to follow his ski tracks back whilst we can?' I said.

He nodded. 'Ought to,' he said. 'There's his sister—she'll want to know. And the Studios will expect a full report. The blood will show us the trail, even if we can't pick out his ski tracks immediately.' He walked over to the desk and looked at the sheet of paper in the typewriter. He nodded his head slowly as he read it. 'Perhaps that's what brought him back.'

'How do you mean?' I asked.

'Wanted to make certain you'd write the full story for a film,' he replied. 'He'd a great flair for knowing what the film-going public wants. He knew they'd like this story, and he didn't want it wasted.' He picked up a rubber and began tearing it methodically to pieces. Though he had not been a friend of Engles', I think his death had affected him more than he would care to admit.

'I never liked him, you know, Neil,' he murmured, looking down at the dead body. 'He wasn't a man you could really like. You could admire him. Or you could dislike him. But it was difficult to like him. He wasn't the sort of man who made friends easily. He lived on excitement. Everything had to be whipped up—conversation, work, action. That's why he drank so much. His nerves needed the sense of exhilaration drink could give him when there was insufficient excitement.'

'What are you trying to say, Joe?' I asked.

He looked at me then and tossed the broken rubber into the waste-paper basket. 'Don't you see—that's why he came out here. It wasn't a sense of responsibility because he had recognised Keramikos as a Nazi agent. It was his craving after excitement. And because he believed there might be the story for a film in it. And that's why, when he came in here, he sat down at the typewriter and wrote down the title and your name underneath. He knew he was finished. But in spite of the pain, his brain still functioned clearly and he saw what a film it would make. Pity he missed the fire scene. He would have liked that.'

He paused for a moment and stared vacantly at the electric fire. 'It wasn't natural for him to sit down at a typewriter, you know,' he went on. 'Normally he'd have talked. Verbal self-dramatisation was his hobby. But he wanted the story told with himself as the central figure. He saw himself as—*The Lonely Ski-er*. He had to make sure you'd see it that way. He knew it was the end. And he planned his exit as he struggled through the snow.

He wanted an audience. He always needed an audience. And he wanted to die, sitting at a typewriter with a cigarette dangling from his lips, typing the title of the film and your name underneath. It was the thought of that scene that kept him going. He couldn't bear a good situation to be wasted. He had to get back, he had to be sure that you would write the script and that the Studios would produce it as the last work of Derek Engles, their famous director.' He drove his fist into his palm. 'If only I'd not been asleep, I could have taken a shot of that scene. He would have liked that.' He stopped then, exhausted by such an unusually long speech. He was massaging his lower lip between his finger and thumb. I think he was near to tears. For though he had no love for Engles as a man, he had great admiration for him as a director.

I went over to the window and looked out. The moon had set now and it was much darker. Clouds were scudding across the stars. 'Better get going,' I said. 'It looks like snow.'

'Can you make it?' he asked. 'You've had a pretty thick two days.'

'I'm all right,' I told him.

He went out then and woke the porter. Our ski things were in the kitchen, drying before the fire. Before we left, I locked the door of the manager's office and gave the key to the porter with instructions that no one but the manager was to be allowed into the office. 'The man who came in just now has died,' I told him in Italian. 'We will return in an hour or two and speak to the manager.'

His mouth opened and he crossed himself with a scared look. We went out into the snow. After the warmth of that little office, it seemed very cold and dark outside. But there was a faint chill light in the sky to the east where the dawn would soon be breaking. Against it, the mountains towered dark and grim. The wind cut like a knife through our damp clothing and little flurries of powdery snow drove before it.

We had no difficulty in picking up the trail of Engles' skis. He had come down the old Military Patrol track from Faloria. Little splashes of blood showed here and there like crimson pennies in the snow. The track climbed steadily up a sparsely wooded slope. It grew steeper as it turned and twisted along the side of a valley that cut up into the mountains. Once, we passed a big crimson patch in the snow. It was where Engles had had a haemorrhage and had stopped to vomit blood. After that there was no more blood. But when we had climbed out of the wood and were following the ski tracks up a steep slope of tumbled downs of fresh snow, we came upon a spot where he had stopped to relieve himself, and the yellow discoloration was mixed with blood. This alone must have told him that he was seriously injured.

The tracks zig-zagged continuously across the slope now. Once we crossed another set of ski tracks. They had been made by two ski-ers climbing. They were undoubtedly the tracks of Engles and Keramikos, made on their way up to Faloria.

The sky was paling now and the jagged ridges of Tondi di Faloria stood out black against the chill light of early dawn. For such a good ski-er Engles had taken the slope very gently. A few hundred yards farther on we came upon the reason. The snow was all churned up around his tracks. He had fallen trying to do a Christi after taking a steep slope straight. The snow was all trampled about where he had struggled to get himself up on to his skis again, and there were red smears in the snow as though bloody clothing had rested on it. Joe had his baby camera with him, and it was here that he took his first picture.

After that the route Engles had come down became steeper and more direct. It looked as though he had been ski-ing normally, not realising how badly he was hurt, until he took that toss. The tracks were clearer now, for the snow was crisp and frozen and there was no powdery top surface.

In places we had to side-step, for the going was getting steeper.

We were right under the Tondi di Faloria now and, as we struggled to the top of the final snow slope, the whole great line of jagged crests was ranged before us—white avalanche slopes gleaming coldly and topped with wicked teeth of black rock.

Straight ahead of us, across a white, rising plain, there was a gap. The Faloria escarpment finished, sweeping down in a frozen snow slope to the gap. The other side of the gap was formed by the lower slopes of the great mountains that swept up to the Serapis Glacier. And through the gap, rank on rank of cold peaks shone in a watery gleam of the rising sun.

It was up that frozen snow slope to the right of the gap that Engles must have climbed, with Keramikos behind him, for the track to Faloria ran right along the crest of the ridge. Most of this track ran just below the crest and in places the weight of snow seemed to have become too heavy for the slope and avalanches had spilled in tumbled heaps down the precipitous slope towards us, drawing the snow away from the crest.

To our right a long valley swept up towards Tondi di Faloria itself. And here and there in this valley rock outcrops showed black against the snow. The track of Engles' skis ran straight from one of these outcrops to our feet.

We followed the line of his skis to this outcrop. The snow was badly trampled around a jagged point of rock that barely showed above the mantle of snow. 'My God! Look at that!' Joe's voice was awed.

He was pointing on along the ski tracks.

I looked up and followed the twin lines, up and up the slope beyond, to a tumbled mass of heaped-up snow.

The slope reared up a thousand feet or more to the Crepedel of Faloria, a narrow ridge which is marked as dangerous on the maps. The slope seemed nearly sheer at the end. And out of the sheer part of the slope, a mighty avalanche of snow had tumbled. It lay, spilled and disordered, across half the mountainside. And out of the lowest reaches of it, two faint lines ran parallel and close together, as though drawn with a ruler in the snow, straight to the rock outcrop by which we were standing.

Joe had his camera working again. When he had taken the picture, he said, 'He must have been a marvellous ski-er, Neil. He did the impossible. He rode that avalanche on skis and came out of it alive. And then he had to hit these rocks. See—he fell before he reached the worst of the outcrop. But he didn't see that little chap half-hidden in the snow. That's what did the damage.'

I nodded. I was past speaking. It seemed such irony for him to escape that avalanche, only to injure himself fatally on this outcrop.

I was gazing up at the slope, fascinated, when my eyes suddenly picked out a dark object lying on the snow just below the final spill of the avalanche. It was well to the left of Engles' ski tracks, towards the gap, and it looked like the body of a man.

I pointed it out to Joe. 'Is it the body of a man, or am I seeing things?' I asked him.

He squinted up the slope. 'My God—yes,' he said. Then he looked at me. 'Keramikos?' he asked.

'Must be,' I replied.

I looked along the ridge, trying to reconstruct the scene. And then I noticed that, away to the right, the avalanche became indistinct as though fresh snow had fallen on it. 'I think I know what happened,' I said.

He looked at me enquiringly.

'Engles had only eighty-five seconds' start on Keramikos at Col da Varda,' I said. 'I timed it by my watch. The fact that he was a brilliant ski-er would only help him on the down slopes. Going uphill it would be a matter of endurance; and Keramikos, as likely as not, was in better condition. He couldn't have been far behind Engles when they began to side-step up the slope from that gap over there. Keramikos would gain a bit at the bottom of that climb. And then, when he started along the track that runs under the crest there, Engles found his progress blocked by an avalanche. That's an old one at the end of the crest there to the right. He couldn't go back. Keramikos was close behind him and he had a gun. And he couldn't go forward because of the avalanche. There would have been only one thing to do—and he did it. He came straight down the avalanche slope. He was a good enough ski-er to try it.'

'And in doing so, he started an avalanche that brought Keramikos down too?' Joe finished for me. He looked up at the slope again, running his eyes along the ridge. Then he nodded. 'That's about the size of it,' he said. 'Could he still be alive?' He nodded in the direction of the body, lying like a black smut on the white shirt-front of the mountain.

'We'd better go and see,' I said. 'Can we make it, do you think?'

'We can try,' he replied.

It was a precipitous climb. The snow was soft and as soon as we had made any height, we had to pack it down with our skis at each step in order to get a grip on the slope. And each time we trampled it solid, I thought the whole slope would slide away from under our feet.

But at last we reached the body. It was huddled in an untidy heap, its face buried in the snow, one arm broken and twisted unnaturally behind its back. We turned it over. It was Keramikos all right. He was stiff and cold. Only his head was unaffected by rigor. The neck was broken. I took off my gloves and searched through his clothing, which was frozen hard. He had no gun on him. But in his breast pocket I found his wallet. It contained nothing of interest except the statement by Korporal Holt. This I put in my pocket.

We managed to slide the body down to the rock outcrop at the bottom. There we left it to be collected later, and made our way back to Tre Croci. It was beginning to snow again by the time we reached the hotel.

★

And that was how Engles and Keramikos died. And that was how we finished the film, up there on the cold slopes of the Tondi di Faloria.

Before I left Cortina, I made one trip up to Col da Varda. The hut, where so much of it had happened, was a gaunt, tumbled heap of blackened beams, already covered with a light crust of snow. The burnt-out ruins had spilled right over the concrete housing of the *slittovia* plant. Mayne, who had bought the place, left no will, and I fancy the place has reverted to the Italian Government.

Nearly a year has passed now since the night of the fire. But I am told that the ruins of the hut still lie sprawled over the concrete machine-room, and that the *slittovia* is not used any more.

And the gold? I suppose I am the only person left who has any idea where it is. I think I know. But I'm not certain. And anyway I have no interest in it. It has been the cause of too many deaths already. If it is there, then let it lie and rot with the rest of Col da Varda.

THE END